STRENGTH OF SUFFOCATION

AN INSPIRATION TO MOVE

PURNA PRADHAN

© **Purna Pradhan 2019**

All rights reserved

All rights reserved by author. No part of this publication may be reproduced, stored in a retrieval system or transmitted in any form or by any means, electronic, mechanical, photocopying, recording or otherwise, without the prior permission of the author.

Although every precaution has been taken to verify the accuracy of the information contained herein, the author and publisher assume no responsibility for any errors or omissions. No liability is assumed for damages that may result from the use of information contained within.

First Published in November 2019

ISBN: 978-93-5347-904-6

BLUE ROSE PUBLISHERS
www.bluerosepublishers.com
info@bluerosepublishers.com
+91 8882 898 898

Cover Design:
Deepak Lal

Typographic Design:
Namrata Saini

Distributed by: Blue Rose, Amazon, Flipkart, Shopclues

About the Author

Dr. Purna Chandra Pradhan as a progressive man in his life has achieved his B.Sc degree in First Class Honours (Chemistry) and Distinction (Physics and Mathematics) in the year 1980. He has done his M.Sc (with Organic Chemistry and Biochemistry as special paper) in 1982, M.Phil (Organic Synthesis as special paper) in 1984. He has qualified National Educational Test (NET)-1985 in Chemistry conducted by the UGC, India and was awarded Ph.D by the Sambalpur University, India in the year 1988 with thesis titled,"Studies on Heterocyclic Compounds" in which Prof. G. R. Newkome of University of South Florida, Tampa, Florida, USA was one of the examiners. He has completed two years (1989-1991) of Post Doctoral Research in a very challenging field like "Synthesis of C-Nucleosides, C-Nucleotides and Evaluation of their Biological Properties as Potential Drug".

He has been honoured with Young Scientist Award in 1997 by the Orissa Chemical Society where he is a life member. He has published several research papers in Indian Journal of Chemistry and Journal of Indian Chemical society. He has presented papers in quite a good number of National and International Seminars/symposia/conferences. He has completed more than thirty years of academic service as Lecturer, Senior Lecturer and Reader in different colleges under Government of Odisha.

Dr. Pradhan wishes a unique place in the society which could be his recognition. He is not at all a free species all along his life so far. He is bound by certain limitations of his choice. By keeping himself within the purview of these restrictions, he has almost failed to find immediate accomplishment. With these failures he has tried to have acquired a little success after spending a lot of interest, energy and time in overcoming too many odds and oppositions. He, therefore, enjoys his finding though less in quantity and/or quality.

Disclaimer

The publisher has fully tried to follow the copy right law. However, if any work is found to be similar, it is unintentional and inadvertant and the same should not be used as defamatory or to file legal suit against the author/publisher.

If the readers find any mistake/s, they may kindly point out those to us and we shall gratefully correct them in the next edition.

To the Memory of my Parents

> "Stretch your arms as per the length and breadth of the blanket of our village life. Village is beautiful, simple, honest and cooperative to sustain society. There is a lot of work to do for village. When village laughs the country and beyond will laugh. There is purity, pleasure and peace in village. We love our village."
>
> *Agadhu Pradhan (Father)*

When we look at the cerulean sky, the desert, the sea or even close our eyes and think for a while, many things come to our mind. Have we ever tried to concentrate on these ? Like seven colours fused in white sunlight, there is something transparent and concrete in the core than that what it appears at the surface. The regular handy sewing work of my mother in more than a month's period under the dim light of a small kerosene lamp at about 4 am everyday in my presence for four to five rupees is unforgettable. My honest and simple parents in their hamlet behave very naturally in every pace of their thought and work. I love it. I adore them for their simple and rustic life far away from the madding crowd of the urban milieu. In addition to farming, my father's low-wage hard earned carpentry for the family, I used to watch occasionally from a close distance. His perseverance in agriculture under the scorching heat of the sun, the chill of winter and sometimes in severe downpour is still green in my mind. Their hard-fought daring deeds have provided me inspiration to conclude that there could be something for which one does not hesitate to take pain. There could be something for which a camel eats thorny plants with its own blood at mouth while chewing. Like repulsion, the real test of electricity, obstacle is an avenue for progress. Pain brings success of pleasure and serenity of mind.

My book, "Strength of Suffocation : An Inspiration to Move" is a feeling of mine that I wish to share with others and dedicate it to my parents for their unflinching faith in God and love for idyllic rustic life. It is a creation of my unflagging inspiration to go ahead even in difficult and trying situations. With this offer, I pray before the Almighty for the peace of my dear departed : the two sacred souls whom I shall cherish in my mind for ever.

Purna Pradhan

Foreword

Sd/-(Dr Gopabandhu Behera)
Former Professor and Head,
P. G. Department of Chemistry,
Sambalpur University, Jyoti Vihar,
Burla (Odisha), India – 768018

Dr Purna Pradhan has presented various scenarios where 'suffocation' is used for the quest of knowledge, for ones aspiration, for encouraging one to accept failures as stepping stones to success. Usually suffocation is the uneasiness of a person in a reduced oxygen atmosphere, but here the author has emphasized how 'suffocation' in human beings can solve problems of pollution, can make them not merely educated but wise, etc. He has elaborated the idea using various situations including his own life from childhood days to his post retirement period.

Every human being feels suffocated in a particular environment. In that case he or she either changes the environment or changes himself or herself to adjust to the environment. Dr. Pradhan has elaborated the first option with various examples.

This book will be an interesting piece of reading material for young generation particularly for the students of various levels. The author could have many more examples from all branches of science where greatness has been bestowed on people who have felt suffocated and have made efforts to come out of their 'suffocation'.

I congratulate Dr Pradhan for developing an idea into a book.

Sd/-(Dr Shyam Prasad Swain)
Former Principal, Associate Professor in English and Head Department of English, Gandhi Mahavidyalaya, Rourkela, Odisha, India-769004

Dr Purna Pradhan deserves to be eulogized for taking up a theme which is relevant to Zeitgeist, a topic which teaches as it delights. It is a simple philosophy of living, a book that will indubitably transform our lives. The book posits simple wisdom that anyone can benefit from. Dr Pradhan imparts a greater sense of meaning, happiness and fulfillment to the readers. His book radiates a unique positive energy in a very passionate and pragmatic manner and beckons the readers towards a world of enlightenment. Quite motivational in his arguments, Dr Pradhan has a lucid down-to-earth way of ventilating his powerful vision for a better living and life-style. He aims at providing the readers with a scientific insight so as to make them a man of the world who can weather all tensions and maintain equipoise in his ordeal of life.

Sd/-(Anchintya Narayan Jena)
Associate Professor in Zoology and Head Department of Zoology, Dalmia College, Rajgangpur, Dist.-Sundargarh, Odisha, India

"Strength of Suffocation : An Inspiration to Move" is an expression of perseverance in the face of daunting challenges. The history of civilization and human progress is the history of immense courage and creativity in encountering the big wall of hopelessness, insurmountable difficulties and unimaginable odds.

The author has depicted his personal toil and the struggles of people around him, who faced odds to spread happiness and hope all around and has given a roadmap for a better future for the humanity.

Sd/- (Pradeep Kumar Mishra)
Reader in Political Science,
Municipal College, Rourkela
Odisha-769012, India

"Strength of Suffocation: An Inspiration to Move" vividly depicts the author's inherent feelings to transform his thought into an idea of building up a better future for humanity. The book manifests The Mother's voice of positivism which says, "When it appears that everything is lost, in fact, all are saved". It has also the traces of Gandhian ideology that science without humanity is pernicious. The author has expressed his concern about relentless scientific developments devoid of fundamental tenets of humanism. The book will be a source of inspiration to the readers to explore the mysteries of Nature and contribute their best selves to preserve its pristine purity for the posterity.

Sd/- (Dr. Hemanta Kumar Mishra)
Associate Professor and HOD of Physics,
S.A.Mahavidyalaya,Balipatna,
Dist.-Khordha, Odisha-752102, India
Phone (91) 9437168168
Email: hkmphysics11@gmail.com

Dr Purna Chandra Pradhan-a stoical, contemplative yet pleasant scientific philosopher has always been an inspiration to his students, friends and others by his own achievements and failures leading to success. His promethean creation, "Strength of Suffocation (SOS)- An Inspiration to Move" is an extraordinary perception of cerebration on fantods of adversity, languish and affliction which usually suffocate a normal human being in his or her life time. The prodigious optimistic approach of conversion of suffocation to strength has been explicated in this book as a clarion call of inner-self while fighting ceaseless battle against the depraving factors as well as the inner and outer enemies. The quintessence of various articles demonstrated through practical experience and paradigmatic examples of SOS, are quite exhilarating. In the rubric to introductory commentary, it can be said that, the book is going to give an impression on the minds of readers to rethink on suffocation and the fetters of life and help them for their physio-psycho development.

Preface

"I've missed more than 9,000 shots in my career. I've lost almost 300 games. 26 times, I've been trusted to take the game-winning shot and missed. I've failed over and over and over again in my life. And that is why I succeed."

Michael Jordan

I felt weak and embarrassed when I saw one of my friends requesting me to write a book. Then and there, though optimistic, my reply was not positive. Much later with a belated response, I thought what I should write. Soon after my superannuation on 31st January 2019, it was at least certain on the surface that I would write something. As I love Organic Chemistry, people around me were expecting a book on Organic Chemistry from me. However, I could not get any call from within to meet their expectation till I reached the age of sixty.

In a TV screen, one day I saw a boy being sunk into water and struggling for survival. This incident provoked me to write the book, "Strength of Suffocation : An Inspiration to Move" because I am engrossed in variegated thoughts and always remain suffocated for something that has become an inspiration for the next. I am sunk in troubled waters. I continue to feel this as an occasion that does not come over and again in life. Sinking into water is a common incidence, but to visualize a book through it is unique. I caught hold of it very tight and tried to cash on it.

Unless we fall we can not stand, unless we sink we can not learn swimming. Unless we are tested we can not justify.

When I thought of writing this book, I felt unskilled and insufficient but never nervous against the inner urge for the task. So I prayed Providence to give me strength and show direction. When I turned out pages of my life so far I found failures and failures. I could not find a point from where I would start. Any way, I took an attempt to collect the list of failures which may provide a spark to enlighten the venture. In fact, I could not be a good teacher or a good researcher, what at least I have had in my life. I do not know whether I could be a writer to whom people would like to read. I believe that we are what we choose to be. Nobody is going to come and save us. We have got to save ourselves. Nobody is going to give us anything. We have got to go out and fight for it. Nobody knows what we want except us. Nobody will be as sorry as we if we do not get it. So, let us do not give up our dream.

Our face is a preface of what we are. Life on earth is a prologue to life elsewhere. This book has emerged as a preface to so many instances of so many people in so many walks of life. Through Nature we are to collect experiences and emotions and apply these for the benefit of the living system in general and human in particular. So let us keep our face clean and plain so that everybody can know what we are. Let us keep our planet clean and conducive to human progress so that this life on earth will continue to prevail in the days to come.

The maiden edition of this book has evolved out of repeated failures, agony of mental and moral torture against higher ambition. I have never thought to work in a way for such long twenty eight years till my superannuation. With less IQ and more EQ, attempt has been made to impart a tiny spark of light what has been produced after being burnt severely. This book is written for the people who decline in self-love, self-confidence, self-respect, self-sacrifice and self-faith in God. From a message of The Mother, "When everything appears as if lost in fact all are saved". It is said, "Failure defeats losers but inspires winners." In my view a book is written neither to get a job nor to get a promotion or nor even to make money. In fact, it is a medium of sharing, transfer of idea and emotion. I will be happy if this book can convey my message to the readers to provide evidence that failure can be a pillar to success.

The various articles have been focused as medium for communication of a message that failure can be pillar to success provided it generates adequate suffocation for something positive possessing interest and energy for the next. Stability of satisfaction brings end to progress. And end of progress is end of life. To open up the various articles tagged in the book, an humble attempt has been made here. These articles have unanimously come forward to spread the message of motivation for motion in situations like stress and strain. If someone is in motion then there is a chance of getting any part of the way to his target.

As many as eighteen articles have been composed to display the power of successive failures. Last but not the least, I preferred to present myself as the living evidence for such a small unusual feeling.

The article, "Industrial Pollution and its Impact on Society" is synchronized with author's feelings with a view to warning and assuring the human society that merciless scientific exploration of Nature in meeting the limitless human desires is slowly and steadily posing a threat to life on earth and side by side passing through a chaotic phase of transition required for a cosmic transformation of life on earth. In fact, it depends on us whether to go for permanent pain and panic through short term temporary relief or permanent pleasure and peace through short term temporary trouble.

I intend to send a signal through the article, "Endangered Basic Science" that unless the basement of the ongoing tower of scientific achievements is made strong it may collapse before the technology of applied science is really applied on basic science. Without basic, we may find mass but not weight, age but not health, qualifications but not education, knowledge but not wisdom, property or power but not peace.

The article, "Science and Entertainment" is aimed at serving as a messenger to make understand and aware of the human society in easy and accessible ways about the role of both material and moral science in understanding Nature, created by God. Science could be brought to mind and body through ways of entertainments. Entertainment of pleasure and peace can come out of science of feeling.

Research is the backbone of development and seminar is an indispensable part of it. It can inspire and increase the potential for progress. It gives a platform to speak and ask without fear. Of the two results of research, 'paper' is broad and open to carry a noble message of sharing while 'patent' is narrow and limited with self centered incentives. With these objectives the article, "A Seminar Talks…" is composed.

With a view to emphasizing on qualitative study the article, "Study by Choice or Chance" is executed. To study by choice is selective and is a matter of taste, again an outcome of so many factors. However, to study by chance, is accidental and opportunity oriented. Whatever, by chance or by choice, once study became passion, the result is positive though may be from a different perspective.

With passion for chemistry, I have not forgotten to focus on the material aspect of a living body fit for sustaining mind and spirit/psyche/soul. I have taken an attempt to display the chemical components in living system and the search for this kind of components to assist in the search for life in heavenly bodies other than the earth. The article, "The Chemical Basis of Life" may provide awareness and interest for a greater quest of finding life anywhere else.

In the exploration of Nature, man is proceeding with science without conscience. It has as if, lost its humanity. It does not care about the selectivity of God in His creation. It even tries to improvise His work for its own comfort and luxury much beyond necessity. A small attempt is made through the article, "Man Without Humanity" to make it public that science without conscience, man without humanity may not be a success for the amelioration of either life or man itself. For the so called benefit from a particular view what science is able to observe may not be the same from overall view that can only be foreseen by God. So science has to adopt conscience before proceeding in its mission.

The article, "Study for the Subject" is a bit of extra care for the growth of subject. In my view suffocation for improvement of the subject is reflected in the article. The subject needs a lot of elevation both in quality and quantity. I feel shy and shame to see the subject undermined by a learner. This feeling is carried in the article.

I want to express my belief in Sri Aurobindo's philosophy on establishment of immortality on earth, i.e., evolution of consciousness of species-evolution of matter to spirit/soul. The article, "Words of Within" happens to be a messenger to spread the message of evolution of lifeless to life (though not established scientifically), evolution of species (established scientifically by Charles Darwin, Frances Arnold etc.) and evolution of consciousness from mental to moral mental to over mental to supra mental. Life on earth so far has witnessed appearance and disappearance. It is yet to establish to remain for ever in spite of the mythological belief on the immortality of Bibhishan, Parshuram, Hanuman and Ashwatthama in the 'Ramayan' and the 'Mahabharat'.

Through different arrangements of lenses man has been able to look into the microscopic world of cells, molecules and even atoms. Towards mid twentieth century the magnetic property of nucleus and its electron environment dependence gave rise to a technology called Nuclear Magnetic Resonance (NMR) Spectroscopy and became very useful to structure determination of most organic molecules. The article, "NMR in Molecular Analysis" speaks in brief the origin and application of NMR in chemical and medical fields. The suffocation of two American scientists, Edward Purcell and Felix Bloch to apply NMR for structure determination of ethyl alcohol for the first time gave additional power to molecular analysis.

Molecular analysis has become increasingly important for a chemist. While working in the laboratory, a chemist faces a lot of difficulties to find a pure compound from a mixture of its isomers. The article, "Stereochemistry – A New Dimension to Molecular Analysis" depicts the possibilities of different stereomers in a mixture. The physical and chemical properties of stereomers are quite often used not only to isolate and identify from the rest in the mixture but to synthesize a particular stereomer with knowledge of stereoselective and stereospecific reactions. A particular isomer is needed for chemotherapy in treating different diseases today.

To compare the concept of "Chess" game with chemical synthesis is an innovation of Dr. Elias James Corey, Chemistry Nobel Laureate of 1990. Hypothetical reverse study of the target molecule to synthons of simple and easily available actual starting molecules (retrosynthetic analysis) and then to really proceed with these starting molecules till the target molecule (Chemical synthesis) are the phases of target synthesis. The real logic in later phase is borrowed from the "Chess" game to block all possible ways but as minimum as one through which the reaction is open to proceed selectively or sometimes specifically. The visionary approach is well supplemented by artificial intelligence and the molecular models. The article, "Retrosynthesis, a Chess Game and Molecular Models" is a model to explain the great idea of Dr. Corey in practice.

Even today, quite a good number of people love the natural ecosystem. Without even much scientific awareness about the necessity of such ecosystem for sustenance of life on earth, they believe that natural calamities like earthquake, flood, drought, global warming, unusual weather change etc. are consequences of the man made ecological imbalance. The article, "The Priest of Nature" would tell us about one of such people who loved education, environment and rural life. He was not only a philanthropist but a priest of Nature. By profession he was a science teacher. He was fond of science, education and environment. So he was ever ready to work for the development of these.

Committed work and man with it cannot die. Both are remembered in earth for ever. It's work in principle or practice is printed on the surface of earth in golden letters. The article, "Young Man of Committed Work cannot Die" describes an example of this kind to motivate people for good work. So, let us not forget to accept that work is commitment, work is teacher, work is worship and work is God so that concept of bad work will not come to mind at all. Here we should bear in mind the dignity of labour.

Soul is noble, however, when it comes to a life through a body on earth it gets painted with the colours like good work or bad work. The article, "A Noble Soul" is created to cite an example of a Noble Soul-a noble personality who has tried his level best to think and work better for others in need beyond his own confinement of a life full of struggles. The path of 'Yoga' has, however, added the flavor of necessity, commitment, pleasure and peace to his life. Training the learners on the roads of a metropolitan city to drive a non-living car, he manages to sustain his family while training to drive a living car (human system) on the path of Yoga, he manages to lead his life.

The article, "An Appeal to the CM" emphasizes on education and research as modes of development. The glorious cultural heritage of the past of the country must not only be followed in principle but also be executed in practice. The suffocation of each and every individual in general and heads of state and government in particular for healthy education and scientific awareness with conscience would bring a radical transformation in the quality of life.

I have wished to add an article on my life before service, within service and after service. Unlike admission into academics as a student (the 1st transition for self learning), exit from academics and admission into service (the 2nd transition-for social service) is followed by superannuation from service and entry into independence (the 3rd transition-for spiritualization). The article, "Superannuation - A Transition in Life" has drawn a line of separation between two eras. Superannuation is not only end of a period but beginning of another period in life. I feel as if the first transition is for self service, the second is for social service while the third period is for socio-self service as a member of the whole human community. In the article I have focused on the origin, evolution and spiritualization of life on earth.

I have tried to behave myself as a living model to justify that failure can be a pillar to success through the article, "Suffocation – A Case Study". The article speaks of my biography of little success through a chain of failures from my childhood till my retirement on superannuation. I emphatically stress upon 'suffocation' of the times since suffocation imparts strength, both physical and moral, for tomorrow's struggle.

Purna Pradhan

Acknowledgments

It is my pleasure and privilege to acknowledge that a book titled, "Strength of Suffocation : An Inspiration to Move" finally came out of a solution of variety of experiences and involvements at a time that I never imagined before. I am in fact indebted to many factors and faculties for their support and co-operation to act as seed in the budding process of the book. I was keen to observe everyday, the stepwise growth of my academic endeavour to crystallize in the formation of the book. The various molecular chapters have been taken care of within the purview of my limited awareness. I would thankfully welcome constructive criticisms and comments from the readers' end and would never mind for adverse reports because that would be my inspiration for the betterment of the book.

These days, I feel as if it is my 'Hour of God' because it gives me ineffable pleasure to get involved in the daily development of the book in terms of planning, programming, seeing and seeking help from viable corners in all possible ways. Though I am determined to complete the work, yet I don't foresee a fixed period within which this could be possible. I leave it to Him. This is not the job of one individual. Moreover, I feel it as a team work that I sincerely and humbly wish to lead. I just persist in moving with this project everyday without a perfunctory break. Hope, God will respond to my effort in course of time.

I would like to extend my thanks to Sri Bhaskar Chandra Dhal, Demonstrator and Sri Bhaskar Chaudhary, Reader in Chemistry for igniting in me the necessary energy of activation to go for a book though it was to be on Organic Chemistry that I love. I am obliged to the opportune moment that struck me with a very positive force to awake the seed of my inner will that has not only germinated and grown but become fruitful. The taste of the fruit whether sweet or sour or in between will take time to come from the readers' end. I continue to convey my gratitude to Sri Achintya Narayan Jena, Associate Professor in Zoology for his constant and continued encouragement for the project and timely suggestions on the biological and philosophical aspects of certain articles in the book. Sri Deba Prasad Mohapatra, Associate Professor in Chemistry became extremely happy to energize my decision into practice. Cooperation of Prof Gopa Bandhu Behera, Prof Ashutosh Nayak and Prof Rajani Kanta Behera (all being my revered teachers at post graduate level and beyond) in this context have added fuel to keep me burning to impart light. It is memorable to mark Prof Behera bothers' delectable and overwhelming appreciation for my zealous interest for this humble creative writing. In fact, I do not find words to express the feeling of Prof Nayak about my maiden attempt for this small contribution of motivational writing. I am indebted to them for their timely response. Dr Hemanta Mishra, Associate Professor in Physics has shown his exemplary attitude with suitable suggestions to boost my energy to a considerable height. So, I am indebted for his involvement in the writing. I am pushed up to express my feeling into words by many persons in general and Sri J. K. Rao in particular when Sri Rao was an Associate Professor in Commerce and Principal, Municipal College, Rourkela, my parent institution where I worked for more than twenty eight years. So, I am very much thankful to him. Sri Pradeep Kumar Mishra, Reader in Political Science has rendered his whole-hearted support for the book and committed in principle and practice for beautification of the book prior to submission for publication. I acknowledge my obligation to him from the inner core of my heart. I am immensely grateful to Dr S. P. Swain, Associate Professor in English and Former Principal, Gandhi Mahavidyalaya, Rourkela, for going through the manuscripts and making necessary corrections and giving valuable suggestions which have been incorporated. Needless to say that Sri Mukteswar Choudhary, Associate Professor in English, has been impressed in my idea behind the book and expressed his good wishes for the completion of my work. I am very thankful for his increased involvement and the meticulous care he has taken in the process of publication of the book.

I thank my colleagues at College of Arts Science and Technology, Bondamunda and Municipal College, Rourkela for their helpful suggestions that they have offered over the period. I sincerely thank my school and college teachers who have come forward to extend their moral support in giving shape to my thoughts, a shape which may be an inspiration for the people in need. I am at a loss of words to ventilate the help which they have rendered from time to time.

I sincerely thank great people like Michael Jordan, Edward Everett Hale, Nathaniel H Egleston, Stephen Hawking, Loretta Lynch, Albert Einstein, Scott Adams, Herbert Spencer Jennings, Elias James Corey, Rabindra Nath Tagore, Charles Darwin, Frances H Arnold, Sri Aurobindo, Francis Crick, Emil Fischer, Nityananda Biswal, Dalailama, A. P. J. Abdul Kalam, Jim Rohn, Ashok Nayak, Suresh Pradhan, Chanakya, Mother Teresa, Martin Luther King Jr. whose photographs with or without message have been placed in various chapters/articles in the book. I specially thank Dr Stewart W Schneller, my research guide in USA for sending his photograph and few words of appreciation and good wishes for this noble job.

I must not forget to include my family members and my late parents in the creative endeavour of bringing out this book. I am thankful to my wife (Kalyani), two sons (Chiral and Biral) and younger brother (Suresh) for providing moral strength of support to complete the book and contribute even a little to those who are troubled and tired to shoot at their targets. But for them my dream of publishing this book would have remained unattainable.

Most importantly, I feel fortunate to have the blessings of the Almighty to see such a nice time in my life. Hope, He will continue to shower His benedictions to keep me alert and active till the last breath of my life. I am immensely grateful to Him-the Moving Pen-which writes and having writ moves on.

Purna Pradhan

Contents

Introduction	1
Industrial Pollution and its Impact on Society	8
Endangered Basic Science	14
Science and Entertainment	18
A Seminar Talks . . .	22
Study by Choice or Chance	27
The Chemical Basis of Life	32
Man Without Humanity	39
Study for the Subject	44
Words of Within	47
NMR in Molecular Analysis	52
Stereochemistry- A New Dimension to Molecular Analysis	57
Retro-synthesis, a Chess Game and Molecular Models	62
The Priest of Nature	65
Young Man of Committed Work cannot Die	69
A Noble Soul	73
An Appeal to the CM	78
Superannuation - A Transition in Life	87
Suffocation a Case Study	90
Epilogue	115

Introduction

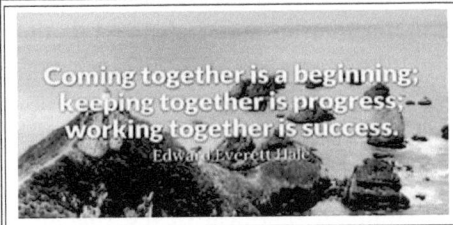 

We inhale oxygen and exhale carbon dioxide for survival, to keep our life on the move. These two chemicals have their specific role in our respiration, from lungs to cells and the reverse through blood. When it is blocked, we suffer from shortage and suffocate for surplus of oxygen in and carbon dioxide out. Accordingly, we try to come out of this blockage. The trial we make is a measure of the extent of our suffocation. Sometimes we succeed and quite often we fail. This success and failure depend on many factors like our pre-state, our environment and post-state of being. Opposition causes suffocation which provides proportionate strength to take the task of reaching the target. Virtually suffocation no doubt is a crucial factor in getting the goal. Suffocation, therefore, brings opportunity that never comes over and again in life to proceed. Dr. A. P. J. Abdul Kalam observes : "Obstacle comes never to harass us but to help us". It beckons us from nescience to prescience.

    The author intends to open himself up before the public through this piece of writing which he dedicates to his parents who with real rustic love never wanted to release him from their reach though love is liberating by nature. This kind of environment in the path of the author's journey appeared as a blessing for a little progress in life. On coming from the pure moral past of the East and moving towards the most developed material West, it appears as if ethics declines with the evolution of matter. We in the East continue to run after materialism while they in the West find occasional interest in our cultural heritage. Quite often, we follow our past procedures and practices but execute their present habit in practice. At this critical juncture, the author persists in his struggle to mould both past and present on a common platform of the Occident and the Orient in introducing ethics in the progress of our self. In an attempt, he remembers his well-felt past to ventilate a few words.

About sixty years ago with a lot of anxiety and aspiration, a baby was born in a rural village, Binayakpur of the then Puri (now Nayagarh) district. His father was a farmer-cum-carpenter. He hailed from a lower middle class family for which his father wanted him to go for a job immediately after completion of his matriculation (Class 11) in 1976. But time perhaps wanted to see the boy somewhere else to support his quest for knowing Nature through science. Therefore, he pursued the then Intermediate in Science (I.Sc) in Nayagarh College, Nayagarh, under Utkal University. After I.Sc, he completed B.Sc degree in G. M. College, Sambalpur under Sambalpur University. Thereafter, he never looked back and persisted in his academic venture and obtained M.Sc, M.Phil, NET and Ph.D degrees in Chemistry one after another to quench his academic thirst for knowledge. He developed a special weakness for Organic Chemistry. By the time the baby had turned to a young boy of about thirty years and developed a special weakness for Organic Chemistry and Chemical Biology, he wanted to join in the war between drug and disease. Year back in 1988 after the award of his Ph.D degree in Chemistry with thesis, "*Studies on Heterocyclic Compounds*" from Sambalpur University he started applying for a post-doctoral research assignment abroad when his parents were reluctant to find him in an alien soil far away from their home. He was very fortunate to misinterpret the lucid ideal words of his father in Odia whose English version could be like this : "Stretch your arms as per the length and breadth of blanket" and his spontaneous response was, "So long as we would be stretching our arms as per the length and breadth of blanket we would be confined to the blanket only". But he wanted to stretch the length and breadth of blanket, to extend the horizon of his little knowledge, to enhance his ability of working both in quantity and quality. So his father's words and his over interpretation to it have provided additional encouragement for his post doctoral research abroad. After some failed attempts to USA, England, Japan and Australia, on 15th November 1989 he finally joined as a Post Doctoral Associate (PDA) with Prof. Stewart W. Schneller of University of South Florida, Tampa, in a research project funded by the National Institute of Health (NIH), USA. Prior to his U.S. mission and Indian Ph.D. Program in Sambalpur University he tried but failed to work with Prof. D. Nassipuri as a Ph. D. Scholar in IIT, Kharagpur. His qualification of NET, 1985 conducted by the UGC remained as if unused. After two years of U.S. experience as PDA, he did not accept the offer of regular assignment as instructor in the same U.S. University. Instead, as a token of love for his motherland, he preferred to return to India and made an approach to Prof. K. N. Ganesh of NCL, Poona (now Pune) with recommendation from Prof K. M. Madhyastha of IISc., Bangalore (now Bengaluru) for continuation of the US work. However, his suffocation was not enough to execute his thought and experience into practice in a national level Indian Institution of higher repute. So he was forced to continue his earlier work which he had left in Municipal College, Rourkela with very little research facility before flying to U.S.A. Thereafter, he could develop the laboratory there to a synthesis cell, "Division of Organic Synthesis" with internal support of college aid and administration, some UGC funds in the form of minor research project (MRP) and instrumental assistance from Western Odisha Development Corporation (WODC). While doing so with minor UGC research project and trying for higher assignment in higher institutes like universities, NITs, IITs and few central government institutions with higher project with a lot of painful oppositions he reached his senior citizenship on 31st of January 2019. As ill luck would have it , this drowning boy could not suffocate adequately to gather the necessary strength and collect assistance from a rescuer to overcome the opposition for the most wanted and essential assignment and before something happened above water he and his interest were buried below the surface of water till date. Verily opposition gives inspiration and earns extra pleasure when one overcomes it. On the contrary, the zeal for success is a warning that in few cases becomes a frustration but in most cases an inspiration.

God is really great. His curing and healing power from above and our suffocating call from below are matters of human cosmos. Thanks to Him that He has sent him as a man, a much developed creature on earth and has given him ample opportunity to know a negligible bit of His creation through science as a vital instrument. But he is limited to a very lower range, yet to establish as worthy worker of

Him. He sees science confined to matter only. To him, it is the path to spiritualism and self realization through the evolution of matter. God's creation has both living and non-living components. Science as an instrument has the responsibility to explore Nature with a view to serving His will and intention. Our suffocation for right service for a right cause in a right path will not only support His desired design but deliver us from ignorance to wisdom, salvage us from the wreck of existential chaos.

In response to the inner voice, in the afternoon of his life, he (the author) has tried to respond to it through a piece of writing titled, "Strength of Suffocation : An Inspiration to Move". Initially he felt worried to know the ongoing brain drain of his country since his childhood. Quite a few years ago after IT revolution he was temporarily relieved to listen the reverse brain drain of his country. But the mind set-up of most of his citizens abroad is so compact, that they have perhaps no time to look back when they see the western world. In this context, he has his respect for those Indians like Dr. Vikram Sarabhai, Dr. A.P.J. Abdul Kalam, Dr. Homi Jahangir Bhaba, Dr. C.V. Raman, Dr. Srinivas Ramanujan, Dr. C.N.R. Rao and many others who could have earned fame abroad if wanted, but instead, they preferred to serve their motherland and managed to remain in the hearts of many million Indians. In contrast, he feels sorry for people like Dr. Hargovind Khorana, Dr. Venkatraman Ramakrishnan and many others despite their achievements in life. The suffocation of Pt. Jawaharlal Nehru, Sri J. R. D. Tata and Dr. Homi Jahangir Bhaba for a strong foundation in science and technology has made India recognized by world power today. The untiring effort of Dr. Vikram Sarabhai as a visionary pioneer in the space technology has in fact given Indian wings the energy of fire like Dr. Kalam to fly in the missile program of our country. The young boy, therefore, develops sincere gratitude for Japanese, Germans, Russians and Americans and citizens of few other nations in general for their love of their motherland. Moreover, the visionary suffocation, untiring effort and ability of Sri Narendra Damodardas Modi, Honourable Prime Minister of India at present find no comparison to dream India to a very high altitude where many of the problems of this country could be minimized. His suffocation for "Subka Saath : Subka Vikash" could find solutions to many confrontations with this little planet.

This book has precipitated from a solution of Indian base that continues to face many challenges like (i) protection of unity in diversity, (ii) poverty, (iii) illiteracy, (iv) brain drain, (v) population imbalance, (vi) dishonesty (vii) lack of patriotism (viii) deterioration of ethics, (ix) emotional and psychological black mailing of sadhus, (x) freedom of the country from the hands of big bulls etc. Thus, India now needs scientists, technologists and leaders of its own. Through this book that boy-this superannuated man would like to express his love and respect for those who try to elevate the subject in which they work, like to be a son of their soil and love their work and run with an ethical bent of mind.

He wishes to include them who have an impact on his life. His parents, wife, two sons, brothers, sisters, teachers, limited friends have come as catalyst or promoter to accelerate or enhance his journey so far. Their favour as blessing and opposition as inspiration have encouraged him to go ahead with a sinusoidal curve. At this moment he is pleased to remember some of his teachers, Sri Narayan Mishra Rajguru of primary education, Sri Padma Nava Mohapatra and Sri Madan Mohan Dash of M. E. Educarion, Sri Sachidananda Mishra, Sri Basu Dash, Sri

Prafulla Chandra Dash, Sri Subala Rout, Sri Birupakshya Tripathy of High School Education, Sri Mahendra Padhi, Dr Satyaban Jena, Sri Nirod Kumar Mohanty, Dr Rajani Kanta Behera, Dr Gopa Bandhu Behera, Dr Ashutosh Nayak and many others of Higher Education.

Matter is solid, even with a large empty space inside, rigid even with a great motion inside. We are never alone and isolated or neglected. We cluster huge in quantity and quality. We have our strong foundation of the cultural heritage. We are all parts of God. Every individual small or big has something to learn from others. Let us share our feelings of failure and success to ignite the Divine Power that we are blessed with. If we really suffocate to share and adequately try to come out of the opposition with undeterred faith and reliance on self, there is someone to come to our rescue and some way to eradicate many of the problems of our country. We will be able to achieve this through perseverance and endurance. Hope this book shall be an inspiration to one and all and shall aspire to a noble mission with a holistic vision.

* * * * *

Industrial Pollution and its Impact on Society

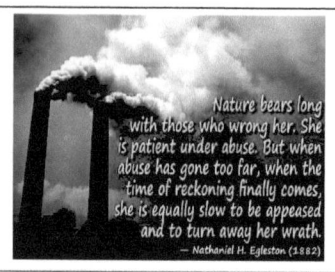

Don't we feel suffocated from too much of dust or oxygen cut off in air ? Have we ever felt suffocated for pure air necessary for breathing ? Have we ever felt suffocated for pure water or soil necessary for living system on earth ? Have we ever felt suffocated from the deterioration of conscience and character in man ? If yes, what have we done so far when our air, water, soil even mind are slowly and steadily going away in quality from that what is necessary for living a healthy life ? Who is responsible for this unhealthy environment for us ? It is certainly we the human beings. To fulfil our unquenching thirst, we utilize science and technology to have both pleasure and problem. In the name of solution to one problem we create many other even bigger problems knowingly or unknowingly. In the name of competitive comfort and self reliance we have earned anger and enmity. We forget that the entire world is a single family. The countries are like its children. Nature and its living mechanism are so subtle and sensitive that any sort of change in the environment, the hydrosphere, lithosphere and atmosphere of our biosphere has an impact on life in both quantitative and qualitative measures. The human mind set-up is geared towards sustenance of life in general. The ecological balance of Nature is disturbed. The living system is being affected slowly but appreciably and steadily. That is what we see today. Ethical bent of mind could provide a solution to this problem and would not allow further degradation of this fragile biosphere. The ultimate fate of humanity may rely on whether we cultivate a deep sense of self-restraint finding non-material enrichment.

The devastating effect of atom bomb has proved more than expected from Nagasaki and Hiroshima bombing. World is really afraid of this tremendous power of nuclear energy, hence taking the plea of not going for it first. In spite of the fact that it is under control, the fear of disaster out of it is always lurking over our head. This could be the reason for which Albert Einstein had to realize that he committed a blunder by inventing atom bomb. In the name of self defence in case of probable offense from outside, countries are marching towards mass destruction by developing both offense and defense capabilities without limit. By the way, not only the biosphere suitable for life has got polluted but also human value has been eroded drastically. Stephen Hawking has warned, "Technology has advanced in such a pace that this aggression may destroy us all by nuclear or biological war".

Man is a social animal. With the advent of its most developed brain and the complex combination of body, mind and soul, it is doing many things today that have started questioning its own existence on earth tomorrow. With the aid of modern science and technology man has been trying to explore the recesses of Nature-the vast but secret source of knowledge without even a little pity for it and apply these for its own immediate benefit and comfort without caring for its after-effect on the living system. As a result, the environment is becoming less and less conducive for life on earth. Now, the ecological balance is at stake. Life is endangered. Many species have become endangered and many are extinct. Let us, therefore, try to save life by shaving this ecological imbalance of Nature.

An undesirable change in the physical, chemical and biological characteristics of the environment that may be detrimental to human and other biotic life is called pollution. In addition, an undesirable change in the environment that affects the moral characteristics of the biotic life is a subtle part of pollution that hampers the value of life on earth. The ethical orientation of mind is now necessary for the evolving life. With so much of temples, mosques, churches, gurudwaras and the like, why the situation of society we see today is so poor. Thus it appears as if the society lacks worshippens and their worship, not temples or so. What I mean to say is that there is a lacuna in the mind set-up today to take up the matter in a non-material but ethical way. Environmental pollution is first a mental problem, then physiological and physical.

In order to meet the growing needs of human beings, "Industrial Revolution" has emerged. Consequently, poisonous particles are thrown into the atmosphere causing dangerous acid rain, ozone depletion, green house effect, global warming etc. Industrial growth and development, therefore, pollutes the atmosphere that affects human life and society very badly. As a result of the presence of certain chemicals the dissolved oxygen (DO) is falling below while the chemical oxygen demand (COD) and the biological oxygen demand (BOD) are escalating the limits meant for plants and animals in water to affect their aquatic life. Due to increase in the amounts of acidic, basic chemicals and non-biodegradable materials in soil, the fertility of the soil is reduced. In an industrially polluted environment, the average age of an individual might be increased because of some life-supporting artificial means, but what about the average health ? Certainly, it is deteriorating. Thus industrial revolution is never made sustainable so far for the living community. The industrial-environmental pollution problems have made us suffocated from poor supply of pure air, water and soil necessary for our biotic life. This suffocation has become the strength for us to struggle today for a better solution of tomorrow. World community is very much concerned about it. So, green technology is stressed upon everywhere. Sustainability for living system has become the basis of consideration of any technology to be applied for any sort of revolutionary change towards meeting human needs. In addition, it has become necessary to see the revolution whether it is accompanied by the evolution of life through possible walks of ethics or not. Despite this effort, there are conflicts in finding it in a common platform throughout the world. Western developed countries point their fingers to the eastern under developed ones to adopt green technology and cut down Green House Gases (GHGs) like carbon dioxide and Chloro Fluoro Carbons (CFCs) like Freon first in the plea that they have brought biotechnology first to the world. On the contrary, the latter ask the former to do the same first for they have the biodiversity. No one is trying to compromise its comfort whatever available, rather putting pressure on the other to go back on the plea of several ways of escape. Unless this attitude changes, life on earth shall continue to be in danger.

Yes for the pleasure but no for the pain in the polluted world today

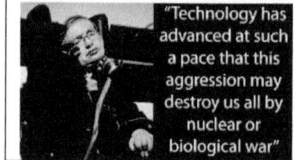

"Technology has advanced at such a pace that this aggression may destroy us all by nuclear or biological war"

Stephen Hawking, a legendary theoretical physicist of 21st century, a living example of suffocation

Solution is confined to words only, not seen in work so far.
The danger of mass destruction is overhead.

A society is a group of individuals with certain objective and constructive attitude. Air, water, soil and noise pollutions that arise from steady industrial phenomena and mind pollution that results from depreciation of ethical bent of mind pose threat to both human and non-human society. In a polluted environment, the society is getting polluted with pollution in the society. The most conscious man gets diseased in both body and mind. Then there comes a change that affects the human value. As a result, hazardous social problems like corruption, theft, irrationalism, terrorism etc. have in fact, become rampant today. The society is disordered and defunct. The human quality and character are degraded. Ethics has gone to hell. No one has time and taste to think whether right or wrong, justified or not. The purpose is to reach the target, irrespective of the path. The only aim is unshared self establishment without caring for others. So, man, its society and nation become selfish which is never good for the entire world. The barbarism in man seems to have surpassed human values. The entire state of man and its society are in chaos. With this kind of present, let us be patient to continually look at the future and feel as if we are in transition, a must needed step for change towards stability and peace. Let us not be reluctant to remember and rely, that cosmos comes out of chaos. The works of matter and spirit we are yet to be reconciled. So, with undeterred faith in God let us continue to suffocate from these for an apt change and realize that this suffocation would be our strength. We have to capitalize on it. So, better try to be conscious and make others conscious of this finding. More importantly, we have to ignite our own strength under the auspices of the Almighty and leave the result to Him. Our effort is certainly going to add. So, let us keep on adding.

* * * * *

Endangered Basic Science

> We all have a responsibility to protect endangered species, both for their sake and for the sake of our own future generations.
>
> ***Loretta Lynch***

Basic science has its ethical sense. It is to survive and grow. It is to explore the mysterious facts of Nature and then technology, the applied science works for the benefit of human in particular but life in general. It has to maintain its survival and growth in suitable and sustainable environment. It is primarily taught by the teachers and researchers. When there is slogan like, "Save environment from its pollution", can we not move further to think and act in saving the society from its corruption, in saving the character from its catastrophe, in saving life from being endangered and extinct ? We have seen in past the green revolution and the white revolution in agriculture. Now the time has come for IT revolution. Computers have made the job easy, accurate and time saving. However, question arises, what do we do with the time that a computer saves ? Can a computer guide us to introduce or upgrade ethics in mind ? Can it motivate us to make a proper use of time that it saves ? Madam Curie died of her own creation. Human life and human values are dying of human activity. The material-man is forgetting the moral-human, the superman. When basic science is neglected, applied science is stressed upon, the negative evolution of the journey of man to machine, spirit to matter begins. Science is a path to spiritualism and self-realization through evolution of matter. With the advent of Science and Technology, without spiritual realization, man has been exercising power over the suppressed. Competition with other poses a threat of enmity that leads to cold war destabilizing peace and tranquility. Competition, however, with the self brings courage, confidence, pleasure and peace to move forward. This is to be realized and suffocated. Moreover, not only basic science but basic education is in danger. The basic aim and interest of human being is in danger. Today man is afraid of living on earth. Man has acquired the most dangerous power of technology to destroy life on earth within minutes. That is why instead of looking for a suitable solution, man is thinking of possibly leaving earth as fugitive and survive in space village, or moon or any other heavenly body (a project in human mind today) much before the dying moments of mundane life.

Like a building with poor foundation, education without a base is at stake. Today the mind set-up is so peculiar that, it may be possible to survive without education, but it appears as if it is impossible without money and power. Virtually money is a power that controls almost everything in this material world now. As a result, recognition of basic science (education) is declining even though efforts are being made extensively to popularize science at its grass root level. A few are oriented towards teaching or scientific research when teaching and research are dedications to the nation. If, teaching and research are so, then who is going to take care of them who are dedicated to teaching and research ? Is it not the nation-the government, to do this ? Inviting a quotation of Dr. A.P.J. Abdul Kalam, "I could not know when my marriage time came and went away." In fact, researchers have no time to think of themselves. In comparison to the West, we in the East are more affected, if dedicated to the nation because of lack of reciprocation. So, people are rather afraid and insecured to confine to basic fundamental science. That is why, a student when asked, opts to become a doctor or engineer or manager or lawyer or bureaucrat or so but normally not a teacher or scientist. Money and power is considered as the standard of living in our country irrespective of the way it comes. A driver who minds the train is even more privileged than a teacher who trains the mind. Unless humans are made, unless characters are built, unless objective of mysterious Nature is understood, we can imagine what may happen in the coming days.

In fact, what has happened ? What has gone wrong with human mind ? In this critical moment who is going to differentiate education from qualification, value of weight from that of mass, right from wrong and so on ? In teaching sector we have seen education industrialization in the state of erstwhile Orissa during 1980s through reopening of too many general colleges. Again we see in 2010s the education industrialization through opening and capping of engineering colleges, medical colleges and +2 residential colleges. The objective of such industrialization is only money. The exclusive aim of making money causes a lot of chaos in the subtle world. Though co-curricular activity is a part, it can not replace curricular activity, what is being done largely today. What is the reason to run after co-curricular but not curricular ? Perhaps it is due to the fact that in the former there is immediate return of reward or recognition that is not found in the latter. However, suffering is certainly found in the latter (but not in the former) because of inadequate reciprocation. For good work in education there is no reward or recognition, but for even unknowingly done mistake there is certain punishment. Consequence is primary not the objective behind. Objective is primary not the path behind. We do not find reward/recognition to a very good class room teacher though quite a good number of teachers are being awarded by the head of state or country. Mostly good teachers try to hide them while such awardees try their level best to get themselves exposed to the award. This is ridiculous at the back. In spite of all these, for the sake of truth, for the sake of knowledge, for basic science-the fundamental science to flourish and flow in each and every individual, let us be conscious and careful to guide ourselves in a direction that will teach us to derive pleasure through opposition, suffocation, pain but peace and simultaneously make others aware so that we will prove ourselves as worthy creatures of worthy Father and our earth will continue to clap with one hand of plants and the other of animals.

Science and Entertainment

"The Science & Entertainment Exchange is a program run and developed by the United States National Academy of Sciences (NAS) to increase public awareness, knowledge, and understanding of science and advanced science technology through its representation in television, film, and other media. It serves as a pro-science movement with the main goal of re-cultivating how science and scientists truly are in order to rid the public of false perceptions on these topics. The Exchange provides entertainment industry professionals with access to credible and knowledgeable scientists and engineers who help to encourage and create effective representations of science and scientists in the media, whether it be on television, in films, plays, etc. The Exchange also helps the science community understand the needs and requirements of the entertainment industry, while making sure science is conveyed in a correct and positive manner to the target audience."

In studying science by chance or choice, there is difference. Science could be read, remembered, reproduced, revealed and realized at the end. It is a path to spiritualism and self realization. Any thing less, brings distance from science. It is heard that the bachelor population in ISRO, the nerve centre of Indian space research is maximum among the organizations of its kind in the world. The objective is to get more time, energy and involvement in research, the backbone of development. Scientists indulge in research which is impregnated into their mind and heart. This is as if their food and respiration as well. Science in collaboration with technology is trying to meet the growing need of man. By the way, knowingly or unknowingly it is bringing threat not only to peace but also to the very existence of life on earth.

Thanks to God that we are human, the most developed creature on earth which is the only heavenly body known so far to sustain life. Life is considered to be a living machine, a perfect combination of some lifeless complex molecules like nucleic acids, proteins, enzymes, hormones, lipids and many others with specific biochemical functions perhaps powered by some kind of force in a lower, living system and is combination of body, mind, soul, psychic and force in much developed human. Retrosynthetic (often called antithetic) analysis of life revcals that life is essentially having a physical body-a base for the living system. Such a base is materialistic by nature and composition. The mechanistic approach for the construction of the body is extremely selective and is, therefore, confined to a limited sphere for a limited period depending on the environment in and around the body. Life prevails in a body as long as the world within and outside is conducive for it and its processes. Life on earth could be endangered and extinct unless we are conscious and careful of it. In this context, science will come to our rescue. Thus, for the continuous sustenance of life on earth, science and its messages should be communicated to each and every individual of our society by various ways and avenues that are easily accessible to them. To keep the plant-animal interdependent living system and its environment conducive for life, use of science and its applications are to be not only followed but executed. The ongoing Government Yojanas like Swachh Bharat, Cleansing Rivers, Digital India, Green Energy, Smart City etc. are to be analyzed and executed scientifically and supplemented by each and every citizen with smart interest, awareness and involvement in a national scale. The idea and effort could be globalised for greater impact.

Nature is the vast source of knowledge for them who want to know. The slow, steady and secret changes taking place in Nature continuously impart observations to them who have strong desire to sense these. Through a falling apple, Newton could see the gravity of earth. Kekule could see the first cyclic compound through his dream of snakes. Human system is made with a brain whose capacity is limited but not less. When brain starts digging Nature, the result is invention/discovery. A strong desire from mind with active support from body makes brain possible to find miracles. This amazing union for science becomes enchanter and entertainer for us. For a dedicated person, achievement acquires entertainment. For a week-days hard worker, week-end ensures entertainment. For acute hunger, food finds entertainment. For severe thirst, water awakes entertainment. Likewise for an explorer, heart-felt science provides entertainment, pleasure and peace. One can not grow with science without suffocation. So suffocation of today for a better tomorrow can only initiate the journey from today to tomorrow.

No doubt, science is a powerful instrument that brain uses to explore the mysterious beauty of Nature. People have slowly realized the importance of science and its impact on life. To develop scientific temperament, is a fundamental right in India. So, every individual in our country must be scientifically literate by developing scientific attitude in him or her. It is not necessary that a scientifically literate must be a scientist. Scientific bent of mind is first a mental achievement then a physical. Thus, scientific temper is attempted to be inculcated in a person not only in the laboratory but in the open fields of interests like games, sports, dance, drama, music or so. For an old honoured scientist, entertainment comes from science throughout when an innocent child or an illiterate old attempts today to enter into science through the easy entry of entertainment. This idea of inducting science into the minds of the children, young or old is encouraging. Science could be entertainment and vice versa. Science is entertainment when it is felt and realized. In contrast, entertainment is science when it is taught through easily accessible activities as per the interest as above. For this reason government is outsourcing quite a lot of funds for utilization in the easily acceptable fields of entertainment towards developing science and inducing scientific temper into the curious minds. By the way, these minds get the taste of science that would bring them to their target one day and help life continue to prevail on earth in the days to come.

* * * * *

A Seminar Talks . . .

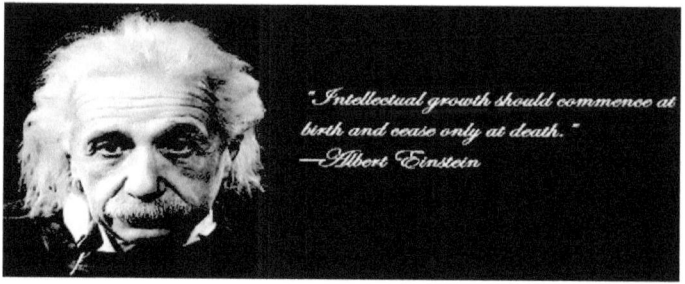

"Intellectual growth should commence at birth and cease only at death."
—Albert Einstein

It is wise to cut one's coat according to one's cloth. But what should happen to the coat when the user grows with time quantitatively and qualitatively ? The coat needs change as per the requirements of the user and hence the cloth. Remembering Charles Darwin, "Survival for the fittest" is a mechanism of natural selection. Man today is striving hard to explore and harness the secret of Nature for its own survival, growth and comfort. With past experience, present expertise and future aim, it is moving too fast with science without conscience to find time and taste for its environment and impact.

Science, like research, is a passion to promises and possibilities. It is open ended like a straight line. Technology like development in the applied sector is cyclic loop like. Research is the basis of development and development is unavoidable to meet the growing need. To keep the development changing and progressive, scientific research, the back bone of development is mandatory. Both intensive and extensive researches necessarily need theoretical and experimental updated knowledge, dedication, love and high level of commitment. The basis of research is creativity. To maintain high quality, scope of science and technology already developed has to be exploited. Open discussion through regional to national and international forum is necessary to make the knowledge interactive and wider. For a newcomer, public exposure through seminar, symposium or conference will provide a platform of opportunity with increasing encouragement and reducing fear, not only to face the challenge, but to get pleasure of even difficult and dangerous work. Immediate use of up-dated information already available is just like a blessing in advance before the next step is approached.

Now-a-days things are getting advanced every second of time. Everyday starts with some thing new. Whatever be the field, it is developing rapidly. The suffocations of scientists throughout the world have no limit for research. Lot of research and studies are being carried out round the clock in various subjects around the world. All these updates on various fields cannot be included in the student curriculum. So, teaching is separated from research at its infancy. As the level of study grows to its youth, teaching and research merge in a common platform of laboratory. The teacher, the taught and the researcher are to move as a concerted team and interact through seminars and symposia. The students have to always keep their eyes on what new things are arriving day by day. That is why seminars are of great importance. Seminars are capable of keeping the students updated with the technologies. Seminars provide latest information about the things which are happening in science and technology. They help in the dissemination of learning. Students cannot improve their knowledge from test books alone. They must take part in various seminars on latest topics. The teachers should also take interest in conducting seminars for their students inviting eminent personalities who have achieved some feat in science and technology. Seminars help the students to interact with the latest scientific trends and the ongoing advancement in technical fields. The educational institutions should take interest in these. Conducting routine seminars among students is also a good habit. This would help to get more information on the particular seminar topic. Seminars also help them to convey their own ideas to their friends and teachers. They will start thinking about new things which they think could be implemented practically. Through conducting seminars they can make others understand what their idea is and how they want to materialize their idea. Another way of properly utilizing the advantages of seminar is to give the students a chance to take seminar on their subject topics. This is turned to be more effective in many educational institutions. Many are conducting seminars of this type. Teachers can always take seminars to their students. It is the old way of teaching. But making students take seminars on the subject related topics would always help them more to understand the subject. This would give them a chance to collect more information about the seminar topic they are provided with. The result is that they would learn the subject well because they have to acquire the knowledge about the subject of their own. There are also many advantages apart from acquiring knowledge. By delivering a seminar talk in front of their teachers, students will be able to talk before a crowd later in their life without any difficulty. Also they can learn their mistakes and can improve their seminar presentation skills. It is actually a great chance for the students to improve their skills within their curriculum. They can improve their language. By taking seminars they will become very much able to interact with the people which will turn out to be useful in their later life. There is a wide spectrum of impressions about seminars. That is why seminars are really a dull way of conveying knowledge at least among some youngsters. But the truth is that most of us could learn the things faster if these are actually demonstrated with some visual display rather than simply read. But unfortunately these impressions may not get stronger if the person who is participating in the seminar is not doing it in the proper way. So by conducting the seminars in proper and better way, the students can interact effectively. It will be the best and most effective way to study. Some seminars have an important role to play in the curriculum.

In the beginning, suffocation for seminar in an institution small or big has to be inculcated at least in one, may be a teacher, or taught or an outsider. With support from others the first seminar is executed in practice. Once students are charged, the seminar will grow like budding of crystal from mother liquor. It is a part of research and academics. It gives platform to stand, strength to speak and courage to carry. When a seminar starts its deliberations, many things happen overtly and covertly. It is an opportunity for the listeners to ask before their fellow-mates and teachers. It is a scope for the speaker to develop the skill and courage for communication, defend what he knows and most importantly to share his thoughts with the delegates.

Unlike an article, or a paper or a book, seminar is a public visual form of distribution of knowledge and information. Visual mode has more impact than audio type. Individual awareness when mutually discussed the outcome becomes not only more but better. Similarly when mutual discussion is made open to a public talk or a regional or state or national seminar or symposium or international conference, interaction is widened among more and more persons of different level. The topic is discussed with greater perspective. Opportunity for national and international interactions opens up. The world will feel like a single community on a particular topic. The delegates will have a chance to share their views more qualitatively with each other. In fact for a researcher seminar is an opportunity to flourish in research activities.

After substantial development in research, most researchers unfortunately suffocate for patent of their innovation. Though **knowledge is free**, yet authors are somehow selfish to try for patent first and then paper if failed with patent. In the former there could be commercial exploitation and capping of the information to a limited circle. Paper, however, keeps its doors ever open to the seeker. Once it is patented, it is closed to others. It is **no more a knowledge**. Therefore, before I conclude, remembering the lines of William Wordsworth in his poem, "Fame and Friendship" I would prefer to say,

Patent is a food that businessmen eat,

I have no stomach for such meat.

But paper is a noble thing,

I like to share with it.

Paper is open to the seminar,

While patent closes its eye.

What can I do more,

Than to say good bye ?

* * * * *

Study by Choice or Chance

"The greatest enemy of knowledge is not ignorance, it is the illusion of knowledge"

Stephen Hawking

A living example of inspiration to proceed in most difficult situations for long 54 years when fell sick of a disease at 22

In the context of the title, it is now necessary to explain a few words involved with a student throughout his learning. Irrespective of time, place, position or personality everyone has to learn from others whether living or not. One is to come in the use of other. This is because all are parts of Nature which is very complex and versatile and can evolve to infinity. This has been felt and believed.

Choice : Life may be likened to a path. We walk along the pathway of our lives, doing our deeds. And sometimes we come to fork in the path where we must choose which way to go. Sometimes these choices are minor which do not really affect our lives much as we continue on the major route. Other choices are major and life-changing, such as what career we will follow. Choice, then, is selection from alternatives. This means we must see the alternatives from which we can choose. Sometimes these are obvious, but often these are not and the path we walk can have a significant random element. Being alert to see the choices we have is a critical ability for living deliberately.

Choosing is the process of selection. Classically, we weigh up each option, considering pros and cons. We then select the most advantageous option. In practice, we are limited by time and the linear nature of conscious thought, so we leave a lot to our conscious minds, which use intuition, rules of thumb, habit and so on. We seldom have complete information and may have to guess. We may also copy others or be swayed by their arguments.

Decision : Decision is a more general term that does not imply the existence of alternatives. It is driven more by needs, goals, and problems than by simply encountering a set of choices. Therefore, it is a process that can vary depending on situation. It can be same as choice, part of choice, generative, predictive, evaluative, more about direction etc.

As per the choice and decision once the target is fixed we continue to pull on well throughout to reach the target. So, decisive people make the decision of their own. They do not get biased. They do not get obstructed too much. Obstruction becomes inspiration and opportunity for them. Normally they do not fail to their target.

Chance : Chance is the possibility of something happening, the occurrence of events in an uncertain situation in the absence of any obvious intension or cause. It is like luck. It is never reliable. So, committed and decisive people do not wait for this.

Opportunity : It is a time or a set of circumstances that makes it possible to do something. It never comes again and again. It is to be recognized, caught hold tight and utilized bravely as and when it comes in life. Once we miss it we find drastic difference in consequence.

A farmer was having three healthy oxen. He had a daughter who had a promise to marry to a person who can catch hold the tail of any of the oxen of her father for at least five minutes. One day meant for the test three persons came as competitors. When they were exposed to the task simultaneously before the first ox, all of them were afraid to catch the tail of the powerful ox with pointed horns. So, they lost the opportunity. Next came the 2nd ox. This time too all of them missed the opportunity because they were afraid of the powerful hind leg back kick of the ox. Finally the 3rd, a relatively weak ox having no such power and organ as above came. All the three competitors decided very positively and therefore, jumped simultaneously over the ox without losing time. Unfortunately the ox was not having its tail.

Ordinarily suffocation is attached to respiration. However, it is the inconvenience in body, mind and sprit to have something one sincerely wants. The unrest, the excitation in between present and future is suffocation. The transition before reaction is suffocation. Progressive dynamism everybody wants. Progress in life makes one lively. Without progress, life comes to an end. Before really achieving we have to first be dissatisfied with the present and aspire for the future. When one sleeps, dream, a psychological state of mind sometime comes. But when one suffocates for something he or she does not have to sleep for dream. In fact the dream does not allow him to sleep. Suffocation is like an explosive catalyst that lowers the activation energy to control a chemical reaction kinetically and make the chemical reaction more spontaneous.

Experiment, observation and inference are three fundamental steps of experimental science. Nature is doing experiments in its microscopic to macroscopic laboratories round the clock. The observations of these experiments are imparted in all directions in wide variety of frequencies and pitches. All observations are not necessarily observed by scientists with limited scope of their sensory organs.

Some of the observations are caught by a growing scientist depending on both the magnitude and pitch of observation and suffocation of the scientist. For example, from the falling apple Newton could discover the gravity of earth. If we really suffocate deeply then our eyes, ears, nose, tongue and skin remain opened and well connected to brain and we sense well. Moreover, the power of sensation through science and sensory organs is limited but not less.

For a growing mind chances are many, may not be in the same form but must be in different form. However, the creation of God is so huge and complex that even though brain has tremendous power, it is not possible to study the whole of Nature. This is because brain is a petty, untrue and incomplete instrument before of Nature. Secondly, the suffocation and span of a life are limited. Hence, it is preferred to go for choice and make the concentrated and concrete use of it. On the other hand, sometimes we get stuck at some point by chance. When the analysis of this accident is made with suffocation to find the cause and rectify or reuse the same for a noble purpose it becomes a choice. Choice is good because one knows it before. Chance is not bad when one is able to make its positive use after. Ordinarily chance as opportunity never comes repeatedly in the same form. However, it may come over and again in different form before a curious mind.

Quite a few times we study by chance that happens under unavoidable circumstances. When environmental need puts adequate pressure to our desire and sometimes we are unable to withstand it and we are forced to satisfy this need. But once we are convinced and engaged in it, something more valuable than the desired may come out either as product or byproduct. This may be treated as study by chance. Madam Curie discovered Polonium by chance from the waste of her work when analysis of waste became his choice. The undesired, unexpected study at one time may be considered as study by chance. However, suffocation after this undesired waste may bring fruit of success by choice. August Kekule had a dream of snakes. When one of his dream-snakes could bite its own tail, he could foresee the cyclic molecules prior to his discovery of benzene, the first cyclic molecule in practice. So 'study by choice or chance' needs suffocation today for innovation of a better tomorrow.

* * * * *

The Chemical Basis of Life

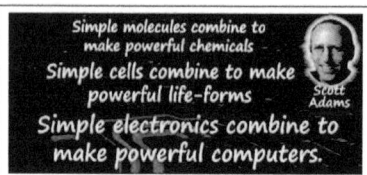 

Retrosynthetic analysis of life reveals that life is essentially having a physical body-a base for the living system. Structurally and functionally such a body is chemical based. The mechanistic approach for the construction of the body is extremely selective and is, therefore, confined to a limited sphere for a limited period depending on the environment in and around the body. Life prevails in a body as long as the world within and outside the body is conducive for it and its processes.

The chemical basis of life is believed when the most developed brain looked into this body. The concentrating and converging journey of uncovering Nature from a body to an organ to a tissue to a cell to an organelle and beyond, has made us understand the structural and functional units of living body-the cells to a small but significant extent of the beauty and mystery of Nature. Philosophically brain is incomplete and always in a state of transformation. So, using brain, a petty instrument it might not be possible to understand the Complete, the Nature what we call God and His creation correctly and completely. However, without caring for this philosophy of life, the suffocating human brain is continually exploring the secrets of life and commanding to have realized the chemical basis of life with an ambition of understanding even the chemical origin of life. Great scientists including Albert Einstein with faith in God and belief in God's existence have made commendable work not only for themselves but for others and moreover for their subjects too. The evolution of lifeless to life and the biochemical mechanism of each and every function in the life processes are being constantly explored with rapidly growing science and technology and the evolving brain. As per a prediction, using only about 2% of brain's capacity science has brought miracles in exploring only about 2% of Nature. We can imagine what we may find when 100 % of brain's capacity is utilized in the exploration of Nature. Human suffocations have no limit now to explore Nature.

Chemistry is the science of the world around us, helping us to understand the make-up of everything in the universe. A series of discoveries over the past few centuries have transformed our knowledge of the world. Understanding atoms and the relationships between them have allowed us to manipulate them, creating chemical compounds to revolutionize our way of life.

To understand when, how, where and why life emerged on earth, science, the brain child of human being is far behind but never away from its ambition. The origin of life is a scientific problem which is yet to be solved. The evolutionary history of life on earth traces the processes by which living and fossil organisms evolved, from earliest emergence of life to the present. Earth formed about 4.5 billion years (Ga) ago and evidence suggests life emerged prior to 3.5 Ga, i.e., 1 billion year after. There are many theories on the origin of life on earth. In olden days, people believed that the universe and life on it was an act result of

God's creation. There was, however, no evidence to support these claims. The early scientists and Greeks believed that life on earth never began on earth itself. They believed that it came from somewhere else in outer space. And they named this phenomenon "panspermia'. Then, came the theory of spontaneous generation of life during the times of Aristotle who believed that life was born from decaying and rotting inorganic matter such as hay, straw and other non-living material. This theory was rubbished by Louis Pasteur. Next came, the 'chemical evolution of life' theory by two scientists – Oparin from Russia and Haldane of England. They believed that the degeneration of life on earth was a slow chemical process which occurred from pre-existing non-living materials such as amino acids, proteins and nuclear material such as RNA. They postulated that these organic materials came together under conditions of high temperature, reducing atmosphere (without oxygen) and gases released from volcanoes all of which were favourable to produce simple living forms. So they called this mixture of organic materials as 'organic soup'. The 'chemical evolution of life' theory was experimented on belief by Miller and Urey in the laboratory. From the findings of the famous 'Miller and Urey experiment' it was believed that mono-atomic units that formed due to chemical evolution polymerized to form polymeric units and that gave rise to the unicellular microorganisms and eventually gave rise to multi-cellular more complex species. This is called biogenesis. Like theories on origin of life there are many theories on evolution of life. The chemical origin of life from inanimate matter has been the focus of much research for decades both experimentally and philosophically. The book, "The Emergence of Life, from Chemical Origin to Synthetic Biology" of Pier Luigi Luisi an Italian Professor Emeritus of Chemistry published by Oxford University

Press provides a lot of information about the chemical origin and chemical basis of life. As per the latest research and review RNA is usually considered to be the first genetic polymer, with DNA a product of a biochemical pathway that arose after the origin of life [Nature Chemistry, 1-6 (2013)]. Understanding how simple chemical mixtures transition into truly emergent systems is essential to create new lifelike materials [Nature Communication 10, 1011(2019)]. The chemical origin of life refers to the conditions that might have existed and therefore, promoted the first replicating life forms. It considers the physical and chemical reactions that could have led to early replicator molecules. Research review (Nature Communications 9, 5174 (2018) reveals that prebiotic chemistry, driven by changing environmental parameters provides canonical and a multitude of non-canonical nucleosides. This suggests that Watson-Crick base pairs were selected from a diverse pool of nucleosides in a pre Darwinian chemical evolution process. Research review [Scientific Reports 9, 1916 (2019)] reveals that the conditions for the potential abiotic formation of organic compounds from inorganic precursors have real implications for understanding of the origin of life on earth and for its possible detection in other environments of the Solar System. It is known that aerosol interfaces are effective at enhancing prebiotic chemical reactions, but the roles of salinity and pH have been poorly investigated. However, it is experimentally demonstrated the uniqueness of alkaline aerosols as prebiotic reactors that produce an undifferentiated accumulation of a variety of multicarbon biomolecules resulting from high energy processes (electrical discharge). Using simulation experiments, it is demonstrated that detection of important biomolecules in thiolins increases when plausible and particular local planetary environmental conditions are simulated. A greater diversity in amino acids, carboxylic acids, N-heterocycles and keto acids, such as glyoxalic acid and pyruvic acid was identified in thiolins synthesized from reduced and neutral atmospheres in the presence of alkaline aqueous aerosols than that from the same atmospheres but using neutral or acidic aqueous aerosols.

Ceylonese-American chemist and exobiologist Dr. Cyril Andrew Ponnamperuma was a leading authority on the chemical origin of life. He built on the work of Miller and Clayton Urey studying chemical reactions in "primordial soup" experiments. Ponnamperuma focused on producing compounds related to the nucleic acids and offered a convincing theory about series of chemical reactions that gave rise to precursor of life on earth. He has suffocated to devote more than four decades in studying to find chemical origin to life on earth.

The journey of exploration from body to its smallest unit has made us aware that the entire body is filled with variety of chemicals with diversified size and structure suitable for a particular function in the living system. Dr. Frances H Arnold, Nobel Laureate 2018 in chemistry claims to say the evolution of enzymes (certain proteins) suitable for different biofunctions as per the requirement. Carbohydrates like glucose provides the energy necessary to run the life processes in human when the same glucose is manufactured by plant, another living system that constantly supports the existence of life on earth. DNA carries the heredity in human while RNA synthesizes proteins-the building blocks of life. Water, the universal solvent serves as the transport vehicle for unlimited number of biochemical reactions. The sodium, potassium ions exchange mechanism of electro chemical actions within a neuron and the transmittance of impulse through the enzyme (colineacetylase) controlled chemical transmitter like acetylcoline and macromolecular receptors in between adjacent neurons against any mechanical stimulus and the mechanical response from the neuron to the muscle tissue are brilliant examples of chemical basis of life. The enzymes, hormones, lipids, vitamins, salts, elements etc. play their unique role in a living system. Hemoglobin in animal and chlorophyll in plant have maintained their crucial care in respiration and photosynthesis, respectively. The beauty is that, life is composed of such lifeless chemicals those coordinate with one another maintaining perfect balance and harmony necessary for life. The life is perhaps something like a power or force that inserts itself into a well coordinated system of chemicals and chemical changes so that the living species generated thereby can undergo life processes like growth, movement, reproduction etc.

The induction of plant-animal symbiosis into life on earth is chemical based. The various bioprocesses in living systems occur through biochemical reactions. Bioprocess is a specific process that uses complete living cells or their components (e.g., bacteria, enzymes, chloroplasts) to obtain desired products. Transport of energy and mass is fundamental to many biological and environmental processes. Nature collects matter and energy from environment to undergo a bioprocess necessary to prepare specific molecules which act in specific biochemical ways for specific biofunctions. The respiration, reproduction, communication and transport, sensation, food digestion, locomotion, growth, the defense mechanism, action-reactions etc. are all controlled or carried by certain specific chemicals. Thus the evolving living system is somehow chemical based. However, evolution of matter to spirit whether chemical based is beyond the scope of this book.

Scientists continue to suffocate to know the evolution of life from chemical origin to synthetic biology and beyond and that is their strength to proceed.

* * * * *

Man Without Humanity

Love and compassion are necessities, not luxuries. Without them humanity can not survive.

Dalailama

Science is a beautiful gift to humanity; we should not distort it.

A. P. J. Abdul Kalam

Man is the most developed creature on earth in the creation of God. He is to evolve to human to superman or superhuman. Without humanity he is just like thinking and speaking beast. Love, compassion and scientific attitude with conscience are among his necessities for evolution in the way ahead. He is a transitory animal. Depending on internal will, external environment and Design of Destiny he would slowly evolve knowingly or unknowingly.

As is realized by Dr. A. P. J. Abdul Kalam, the great Indian scientist, "*Science is an important gift to humanity ; we should not distort it*". However, what it does in addition. We watch today, science has been continually distorting Nature the greatest gift of God mercilessly without even a trace of conscience. What is this and why so ? Is science meant for man only ? Why to create one even small problem and to provide so called solution to it creating many and macro problems ? When is man going to realize and repent for its crime after crime ? Science is no doubt a perfect and powerful instrument to experiment, observe, analyze and infer. But, it is not confined to matter only. It should not forget life's container like body, chemical like brain, catalyst like mind and promoter or quencher like conscience. These are all limited before the Limitless. Thus science is to take care of these to fulfil its not only material but moral objectives.

The average mind setup today is such that man is attracted quickly and strongly towards short and small material gain without even caring for the way and objective whether right or wrong. It is difficult to predict this kind of behavior of mind. On the contrary, man's activity that finds the right result through right route is like mirror in a land of blinds. Such men with such activity are countable to small numbers and do not expose themselves and are considered as if exception or abnormal and, therefore, laughed at by a major community. Human value in man is deteriorating. The march of man is as if backward in evolution. There is no lack of temples or mosques or churches or gurudwaras. Rush in temples or so is more than expected. What could be lacking, it is the worship only. It is strange to observe that right path for right work is normally not followed whereas wrong work irrespective of path and right work in wrong path is generally chased. When there is lapse in humanity, man comes under the clutches of unsocial use of forces like money, muscle, power, position, strength or even sex to go for misdeeds that are quite often happening these days. The weak administrative or judiciary judgment on the accused gets delayed for years. It is like 'Justice delayed is justice denied'. It appears as if laws are not defined well and there are wide gaps among these laws. The width of the gap in certain countries seems wider than that of the law itself. As a result, the genuine is victimized and culprit escapes. Consequently, the victim occasionally loses patience and gets reacted in wrath to commit mistake inviting punishment and pain.

Having ancient base of strong and stable cultural heritage the situation in certain countries is following downward trend in humanity. There is no decrease of viewers for programs like dance, drama, music, cinema or television serial but for the sake of entertainment and amusement only. The power and purpose of these programs is still to be made useful for a better life at the receiving end. The positive impact of these is, therefore hardly observed. The psychological blackmailing by self styled God men is spreading like wild fire in the society. Ignorance, illiteracy and blind belief of common people are instrumental for such spread despite incidental exposure of the fact behind. In the name of entering into modernity, it has become easy to forget the past cultural practices in day to day life. Western use of nude dresses is increasingly followed in the eastern countries. Whereas western world continues to grow with material science and technology, people in the East are far behind. Any way, we find depreciation of humanity in both ends. We don't find examples like 'Harishchandra' or 'Hanuman' today. Instead, 'Ravanas' and 'Kansas' with reduced humanity are increasingly available disturbing social peace and tranquility.

Although automated machines are being used worldwide in place of man for various activities, unfortunately no material machine is yet thought to induce or enhance the ethical essence in man. Science has tremendously increased the man's ability beyond expectation, but of no assistance so far to improve the morality. To get out of too many present crises born of less humanity, it is time to search for solution connecting matter to spirit. To show direction to the deviated man it is necessary to improve his human values. Restoration of humanity can only drive to the Destiny to bring stability and peace. Ongoing education is for knowledge and material gain, not for wisdom or peace that would add to the humanity. The methodology adopted in ancient India to control over the eight bad qualities (eight enemies) should be implemented in educational curriculum of today to enhance human value. Research projects on elevation of humanity should be invited and executed. Possible ways and means to upgrade the human value should be explored.

Man today is less human and more inhuman. He needs to develop pleasure of sharing his own happiness. He needs to gladly improve upon sharing the pain of others. However, he is found selfish and self centered. The inhuman temperament of man is, as if cutting its own branch on which it has stood. The advancement of science and technology with rapid industrialization without conscience and humanity towards Nature for its own survival, growth and comfort has apparently invited an impending danger of environmental pollution posing lethal threat to the very existence of life on earth. Though man has started realizing this fact and reacting to develop green technology and cutting down GHGs like carbon dioxide and CFCs like freon, there is no united international agreement over the issue. Man is not ready to sacrifice its own comfort and dominance over others, hence taking different pleas to escape such an agreement. In this situation, consequence is mass suffering sooner or later. This increasing suffocation of man for self survival and self recognition without caring for the interest of others would prove soon a bane, never a boon for itself. Nature through its experiments has already issued warning of observations that man has already received but trying to shift the responsibility of response in the name of several pleas like biotechnology, biodiversity etc. Man has already been suffocating from the impact of its self made environmental hazards like acid rain, global warming and irregular weather changes causing unexpected tornado, hurricane, flood, draught and the like. Unless man will suffocate for suitable solution to come out of these massacring dangers and more importantly reduce the cause of these consequences at the root, there would be no escape. Man, therefore has to improve upon its human values or else Nature will continue to reciprocate naturally as per its Own Law. Therefore, it would be better to limit the quantitative requirement to help increase the quality of life. The idea of exploiting Nature to infinity should be rejected and instead, Nature may be used just enough to meet the requirement as less as comfortable.

* * * * *

Study for the Subject

The highest education is that which does not merely give us information but makes our life in harmony with all existence

Rabindranath Tagore

Teacher, taught, study and subject are the basic components of education. The qualitative growth of the education depends on all of these. For all round development of education, there should be proportionate growth of all of these. To study for the subject is a creative feeling. When the subject grows, student feels pleased to find a broad and bigger opportunity to grow. And when that happens, the study of student qualitatively increases. This ultimately enhances the quality of teaching of teacher. Thus all of the four are interdependent. If one is in trouble the rest are affected. So, these should come up united as education. When we talk of a subject as vast ordinarily it means that the subject has grown to a very high altitude covering large number of people and large area. In fact education is backbone of internal development. Quality education depends on quality of teaching and learning process, quality of students and teachers. Quality is not necessarily confined to degrees. The impact of quality education, however, is reflected in the society. It brings pleasure, peace and stability in society. It binds people physiologically, mentally and spiritually. When these things happen emotion comes into picture. Emotional attachment does not definitely require any material medium. Again, pleasure in pain and pleasure in sharing the pleasure are Godly.

No subject is less vast. The vastness of a subject depends on our perception and our interest and love for the subject. As a lover of Organic Chemistry the author loves him, his study and his subject, Organic Chemistry. When he finds Organic Chemistry as a subject to interact with he feels elevated even though he has the pleasure of knowing a very little of it. He does not know when and how he could manage himself to entangle into Organic Chemistry. Perhaps his love for living system which deals with a lot of organic molecules has pulled him into this branch of science. Though he was relatively scoring better in Physics during intermediate level of his career, he could see himself indulged into Organic Chemistry subsequently. Immediate after his post graduation in Chemistry he could not accept an offer to work for Ph. D. in Biochemistry because of his special interest in the molecular design and synthesis of bioactive molecules. Slowly and steadily he was pleased to see organic chemistry developing and having a crucial role in life and life processes. Professor Ceryl Andrew Ponnamperuma, a US based Sri Lanka born American Chemist has devoted more than four decades of his span with a view to finding chemical origin of life. Organic Chemistry, the chemistry of most molecules in organs, the parts of living bodies is studied to a very high level. The life molecules such as proteins, carbohydrates, nucleic acids like DNA, RNA and their analogs like XNAs are being employed to trace life in extra terrestrial regions of outer world. Therefore, subject grows when it is studied spontaneously. If the subject is grown enough to a very high altitude, large number of students can see it and it can attract and orient them into it.

The passion for food for a hungry man is compared with the suffocation for oxygen for a sinking one. When the person is hungry, food is delicious. Then the interaction between them is spontaneous and result is attraction, i.e., positive. The suffocation for all round development of teacher, student, study and subject would bring unbelievable result. Our call from below and His blessing from above bring manifestation of education.

As living creation of God, we have the ability to evolve and become Great like a seed can grow to a tree. Universe or multiverse is believed to have come from a point mass after absorption of necessary energy with time. Likewise a seed grows to a tree by absorbing matter and energy from environment. Nature collects matter and energy from environment and synthesizes its requirement. So, proper coalition of teacher, student, study and subject can bring the result to a new height. With analytical and innovative bent of mind one can have a different but better result. When Nature is wide open, quality of study can be very high even in a low unrecognized field of Nature. When student is rich and healthy in desire and determination, study will be followed irrespective of subject. Moreover, higher subject will attract better student and better teacher for higher study. So, we should try with joint effort for the growth of the subject to justify the saying, "United we stand" with developed subject.

* * * * *

Words of Within

Charles Darwin	Frances Arnold	Sri Krishna	Sri Aurobindo	God Bishnu

Charles Darwin to his credit has made us believe the evolution of living species. Of so many theories on evolution of life from lifeless, none is established. Year 2018 Nobel Laureate in Chemistry, Dr. Frances H. Arnold, the Linus Pauling Professor in Chemical Engineering, Bioengineering and Biochemistry in Caltech, USA emphatically claimed to say, "Enzymes are evolvable, we are here because of evolution of enzymes and we can have synthetic enzymes-the selective biocatalysts and exploit these in solving many of the problems of this little planet sustaining life". Sri Aurobindo speaks of the evolution of man to superman, human to superhuman. Thus, there is indication that evolution of lifeless to life to higher life to God could be possible on earth itself through evolution of matter, living species and consciousness. Honourable Bharat Ratna, Dr. A. P. J. Abdul Kalam-the missile man of India said, "Let us dream that which will not allow us to sleep". We can stretch the horizon of our ability with patient interest and involvement. Like repulsion, the real test of electricity, failure before progress, instability as a transition before stability, obstruction appears in the path of progress to virtually help us and make our life lively.

Difficulty and opposition are necessary to enjoy progress and success and to derive pleasure and peace.

Nature is beautiful but complex and compact. Slowly and steadily the evolving man is uncovering one after another the layers of secret knowledge of Nature and looking into it with a view to understanding the truth behind for its own benefit and comfort so far. The timely support of evolving science and its technology starting from the discovery of natural lenses to the invention of synthetic ones have made miracles. One synthetic lens has gone into the sky while the other into the microbes. Thanks to late Albert Einstein and late Stefan Hawking who have reached new dimensions in the field of Physics. Sri Aurobindo Ghosh, the contemporary philosopher and spiritual experimenter of the age has repeatedly said about the evolution of man to superman in his books, "Savitri" and "Life Divine". There are many myths in ancient India about Sri Ram and Sri Krisna who are certainly beyond human consciousness and believe them as representatives called 'Abtars' of God or above. Sri Aurobindo Philosophy depicts Sri Ram as consciousness of moral mind, Sri Krishna as consciousness of overmind below supermind, the complete consciousness.

Today's science is primarily materialistic though scientists have never denied about the existence of God. The concept of dark energy and dark matter is still a theory. Matter exists in metastate, a simultaneous state of all possible states before it is observed. This idea of considering matter appears Godly. Material scientists will be more than happy if they can prove the existence of God like their invention or discovery. The author is in doubt whether the ongoing concept of science can help us in realizing God physically before the brain is evolved completely. The matter based approach of God through the sense of science so far as if draws a line of separation from understanding God, the supramental consciousness. Such a line of separation comes to mind because evolution of matter to spirit is yet to be proved by material scientist. The ancient Indian approach performed by rishies was much more subtle and spiritual than the approach of today's science towards God. Presently man has synthesized many complex components of a living cell, some believe to have synthesized a cell and only away from installing life into it. Man claims to have synthesized biology and is proceeding towards synthesis of life. The installation of life with mind and spirit/soul in a body perhaps requires a different kind of science from what it is seen today. To find energy, the power from recitation of mantras used in ancient age is different from those of fossil fuel, voltaic cell or any other used in current days.

Nature has selected matter and energy from the environment and has made something necessary for a particular operation in biological world. With its classical or quantum consideration science developed so far is unable to replace the Nature's deed. So deviation to Nature's selection may bring accident which may or may not be observed or understood by our ongoing science. For example, pollution of environment is not natural but man made. The international community is, therefore, worried today towards existence of life on earth in future. So, man is trying to utilize all possible kinds of ways and avenues to make earth pollution free and in fact it appears today impossible to the author. However, it may avoid further deterioration in being conducive for life. So, it is better to rely on the saying, "Prevention is better than cure". When we think of scientific exploration of Nature it appears as if science has only science but no conscience. No body knows how long this merciless digging of Nature by science in the name of advancement is going to support the sustenance of life on earth. Scientific outcome is welcomed in one way but questioned in so many ways. Scientific achievement happens to be resource for one but liability for other and is difficult to predict whether it is resource or liability overall. The great Albert Einstein has not forgotten to say that he has committed a blunder to acquire and use nuclear energy in the name of atom bomb even though the key is with us. In fact the key to control man's desire is yet to be made.

In a quantum jump man is thinking to apply green or sustainable technology which is eco-friendly. But, who will give warranty ? Who can correctly read today's so called green technology and certify that it is not red even today or would not be red tomorrow in the eyes of Nature ? Therefore, it appears as if science is in a fix. It does not understand how to justify and meet the growing need of human in a sustainable manner. Should the journey of science from earth to universe and multiverse in seeking life in the form on earth or any other be stopped ? Should we leave the dark matter and dark energy there where these are ? Will it be better to first protect the earth for life on it than to search for life anywhere else with a mission to leave earth in case required ? In the author's choice we should try to protect the one which we are already having not only with the ongoing material concept of science but with the concept of moral science based on ethics and emotion. Research and development should be triggered on moral science what the ancient rishies were used to do. Research methodology should be developed with emotional attachment to understand life on a moral basis. We should concentrate on the emotional quotient (EQ) compared to intelligent quotient (IQ). A more streamlined coordination between plants and animals be established so that they can reciprocate each other like 'munies' and 'rishies' with high EQ in ancient India could know the medicinal value of two unique plants, 'Brahmi' (*Bacopa monnieri*) and 'Bisalyakarani' (*Tridax procumbens*) some 5000 years ago. On the other hand, such medicinal value of these two plants were known much later in early 1980s using much developed science with high IQ in a much developed laboratory of a much developed country like USA.

The past cultural heritage of India be experimented, revealed and revived before the world. The evolution of lifeless to life, man to human and superman to superhuman be realized. Like Newton could see the gravity through an apple falling towards earth, like Sri Aurobindo could see to predict evolution of mind to overmind to supermind in earth, like August Kekule could see the cyclic compounds through his dream of snakes, time has come for scientists to think on conducting experiment on body, mind, soul, pre-birth, post death to connect matter to spirit/soul. Like the transform of matter to energy and the reverse through Einstein's theory of relativity ($E=mc^2$), the route for evolution of matter to spirit be experimented. The whole universe or multiverse if any is thought of as if has evolved from a single point of matter. The philosophy of Sri Aurobindo has predicted that evolution of matter to spirit is possible on earth. Science, therefore, need not be limited to matter. Rather it should be extended to morale and beyond. Science needs to suffocate with conscience for preservation of ecological balance necessary for life and its evolution beyond. As worthy creation of God, let us be conscious and careful all along with sharing and fellow feeling for the growth and development of living system on earth and in addition let us actively involve in the evolution of matter to spirit towards establishment of immortality on earth.

* * * * *

NMR in Molecular Analysis

Almost all aspects of life are engineered at the molecular level and without understanding molecules we can only have a very sketchy understanding of life itself.

Francis Crick

Edward Purcell of Massachusetts Institute of Technology and Felix Bloch of Stanford University shared 1952 Nobel Prize in Physics to have exploited the nuclear property of protium in the analysis of the structure of Ethyl alcohol. In fact, the various energy levels of certain specific nucleus are not only split when kept in an external magnetic field, but under suitable conditions the lower energy nucleus absorbs radio frequency radiation of certain wavelength (depending on external magnetic field strength) to flip to higher nucleus and the phenomenon is called Nuclear Magnetic Resonance **(NMR).** Though the suffocative work of these two Nobel Laureates on application of NMR to determine molecular structure of Ethyl alcohol has raised them to a new height in Physics, it is mostly enjoyed in Chemical and Medical Sciences through NMR and MRI techniques respectively. Magnetic Resonance Imaging **(MRI)**, a modified form of NMR is a medical imaging technique used extensively in radiology to form pictures of the anatomy and the physiological processes of the body in health and disease.

The suffocations of scientists on molecular analyses have brought a lot of technical changes over the years.

Unlike X-ray and Electron Diffraction Studies and spectroscopic methods of analyses like UV, Visible, IR etc., Super Resolution Light Microscopy (**SRLM**) (honoured by 2014 Nobel Committee for Chemistry) and Cryo Electron Microscopy (**CEM**) (honoured by 2017 Nobel Committee for Chemistry) have added new but golden feathers to the crown of Analytical Chemistry. The objective is to view the molecules very clearly in both living and non-living environments and understand Nature through them. Techniques that involve high energetic radiations like γ-ray, β-ray, X-ray, UV-ray etc. to molecular exposure are not useful in living system because these radiations damage living cells. Therefore, determination of structural and functional characteristics of molecules in living system includes techniques using low energetic longer waves like Visible, IR, Microwave and Radio waves which do not affect living cells. To take part in the exploration of living system in other terrestrial bodies besides earth the latter techniques are in use now-a-days.

Coming back to NMR, if the nuclear properties were confined to the atomic nucleus it would be of little importance to Organic Chemists. But instead, nuclear property depends on its immediate electronic environment. What we see, it is magnetically shielded by the local magnetic field caused by the induced electron circulation out of the local electron circulation around the nucleus when kept in an external magnetic field. Thus NMR is quite informative about the local electron circulation around the nucleus, hence the nature of atoms, chemical bonds and thereby the functional groups. The three tier information of NMR absorption peaks provides, (1) the position (called chemical shift), (2) nature of coupling with characteristic coupling constant (J) between protons (called splitting pattern) and (3) relative number of protons (called relative intensity) to identify and analyze organic compounds single handedly to an extent of more than 50 %. Thus NMR is an unavoidable tool for structure determination of organic molecules. ^{1}H NMR, ^{13}C NMR and their combination emerged elegantly the 2D NMR techniques, viz, COSY (Correlation spectroscopy) and HETCOR (Heteronuclear correlation spectroscopy) to identify organic compounds more accurately. Its application in **Medical field** is well evidenced by the much useful **MRI**. Without updated NMR or MRI information, chemical analysis or medical diagnosis is incomplete today.

This article, "NMR in Molecular Analysis" is written to display the continued effort of Purcell and Bloch to apply Physics into Chemistry. The strength they got from their suffocative movements both inside and outside the laboratory to apply NMR to identification of molecular structure like Ethyl alcohol got paid and brought laurels for them and proved a great service to mankind. The credit for the discovery of NMR has in fact gone much before to Isador Isaac Rabi of New Work City's Columbia University, who received 1944 Nobel Prize in Physics for his detection of NMR signal in molecular beam. Rabi's idea of molecular flip to principal magnetic orientation by an oscillating magnetic field was originally proposed by Dutch physicist Cornelius J. Gorter in 1936, a year before Rabi, but Gorter was unable to validate this phenomenon because of limitation of his experimental set-up. Therefore, Gorter is sometimes known as "The man who almost discovered NMR". Suffocation is sometimes insufficient and unable to overcome the difficulty over a period but for a winner it is always strength to success.

The author feels elevated to work on organic molecules in general but biomolecules in particular. What he believes, if Chemistry is considered a sweet, Organic Chemistry is the red topping on it with biomolecules at its centre and he is keenly attracted to such centre. The complex organic molecules or molecular assemblies such as supra molecules, micelles, nanoclusters etc. of today are very difficult to be established structurally and functionally. So analysis of organic molecules is of great concern. In the exploration of existence of life in other heavenly body besides earth, the search for organic molecules like DNA, RNA (or XNA), protein, carbohydrate, fat, lipid, vitamin, hormone etc. involved in the life processes on earth is under way. It is not likely to say impossible for the suffocating and evolving human brain and mind to find life anywhere else either in this form or other. It needs technological evolution further. Hope, this evolving and suffocating human brain will succeed in its search for life with confidence that if it is possible in earth why it could not be anywhere else.

The author is somehow unfortunate to say that the laboratory set-up in the department of Chemistry of Municipal College, Rourkela, his work place is very limited to conduct experiments of his design in synthetic Oorganic Chemistry where NMR instrument is most essential and analyze the medicinal values of the molecules to be Synthesized. All on a sudden he became optimistic to know the installation of a 400 MHz NMR machine in the nearby National Institute of Technology (NIT), Rourkela. The commercial service of this machine became available at his door step. So, he came quick to apply as Principal Investigator to the DST, Govt. of India for a Major Research Project to be carried out in his newly developed research laboratory, the Division of Organic Synthesis (DOS) in his work place. However, it was not enough to analyze molecules of his interest in his own laboratory. His constant and continued effort for the dream development of research in this laboratory will never go vain, he believes. He is again unhappy to say that his state and country though progress a lot but not enough either in quantity or quality or even the rate to compete with international standard. Reasons are many. However, he was not yet disheartened because these reasons are as if in transition which can be overcome to success a day. So, let him wait and watch. Moreover, we must keep on heating and hammering with love and feeling for the nation till it is moulded into shape.

* * * * *

Stereochemistry- A New Dimension to Molecular Analysis

Their specific effect on the glucosides might thus be explained by assuming that the intimate contact between the molecules necessary for the release of the chemical reaction is possible only with similar geometrical configurations. To give an illustration I will say that enzyme and glucoside must fit together like lock and key in order to be able to exercise a chemical action on each other. This concept has undoubtedly gained in probability and value for stereochemical research, after the phenomenon itself was transferred from the biological to the purely chemical field. It is an extension of the theory of asymmetry without being a direct consequence of it : for the conviction that the geometrical structure of the molecule even for optical isomers exercises such a that influence on the chemical affinities, in my opinion could only be gained by nu   al observations.

Emil Fischer

The French chemist Louis Pasteur (1850) was the first to reveal that optical activity at the molecular level was due to an asymmetric placement of an atom in the molecule. He further recognized that enantiomers had equal and opposite effects on polarized light. The first ever 1874 approach of J. H. van't Hoff for the tetrahedral (three dimensional) structure of Methane (CH_4) though opposed by Hermann Kolbe, one of the then organic chemists got overwhelming support and led van't Hoff the first recipient of 1901 Nobel prize in Chemistry. They proposed the tetrahedral model for the carbon as the cause of molecular dissymmetry and the resultant optical rotation. This was the beginning of stereochemistry which emerged with a new dimension and formed a massive and integral part of Organic Chemistry.

Stereochemistry, the chemistry around stereocentre, chemistry with respect to space is a gift of Nature. Configurational amino acids in natural proteins are all of L-configurations while configurational sugars in natural carbohydrates are all of D-configurations. Organism synthesizes only L-amino acids, though at earth's temperature and in presence of the enzyme racemase these are racemised to their D-isomers which are incorporated into certain non-protein molecules. In the living system a particular biofunction is carried out with help of a particular enzyme synthesized by Nature by collecting matter and energy from environment. When molecule of a particular configuration is bioactive to an appreciable extent, its non-superposable mirror image molecule (enantiomer) is not at all. Pyrazofurin (β-isomer) has versatile biological properties like anti-viral, anti-tumor, anti-cancer etc. while its α-isomer is not. In fact, stereochemistry is inducted in Nature much before its emergence in chemical literature.

Stereochemistry deals with spatial arrangement of atoms or groups around a unique centre, called "Stereocentre", a centre (with an atom) so that if two of the atoms or groups bonded to it are interchanged it leads to stereomers. By taking into account the C-C single bond restricted rotation, certain stereomers identify themselves as conformational isomers and are mostly of theoretical importance while actually available conformational isomers called atrop isomers added new feathers to the crown of stereochemistry. With same constitution or connectivity (the sequence of arrangement of atoms or groups in the carbon skeleton), configurational isomers unlike conformational isomers contributed largely to the stereochemical study of compounds in practice. However, with different connectivity isomers are known as constitutional isomers. The presence of geometrical and optical (both configurational) stereocentres gave rise to geometrical and optical stereomers, respectively. The plane polarized light and its use in polarimeter distinctly made optical isomers separate from others. The study of molecular symmetry and its operation with the aid of artificial molecular models in stereochemical analyses are being undertaken quite convincingly. Terms like conformer, asymmetry, dissymmetry, chirality, superposability, homomer, enantiomer, diastereomer, tautomer etc. are keys to analyze molecular structure in three dimensional space.

The suffocation, strong insight and brilliant logic of Emil Fischer proved the configuration of D-glucose with very limited information on carbohydrate chemistry through retro-analytical approach of the possible sixteen ($2^n=2^4=16$) stereomers of glucose with four ($n=4$) stereocentres in each. With complicated polycyclic structures it is often extremely difficult to predict the possible number of stereomers hence equally inconvenient for an experimental chemist to work on synthesis and characterization of a particular stereomer. Therefore, procurement of necessary configuration and stereoalignment of the molecule is a challenge before the synthetic chemist. Stereospecific and stereoselective syntheses have, however, extended their cooperation to assist the experimental chemist in planning, proposing and carrying out practically feasible scheme for target synthesis of particular stereomer. Ernest Ludwig Eliel, a German chemist famous for his book, "Stereochemistry of Organic Compounds" was a professional's professional, academician's academician and a chemist's chemist. At the age of 12, Ernest Eliel was given a chemistry set and discovered his life's passion by creating his own after completing all experiments assigned by his father. To satisfy his suffocating search for knowledge in Chemistry in USA during second world war he had to move to Scotland (1938), then to Canada and then University of Havana, Cuba, Missouri (USA) for Doctor of Science (1946) after enduring rough treatments. As a pioneer in modern stereochemistry and conformational analysis Dr. Eliel has gifted a lot of contributions to the society in terms of scientific articles and reviews, lectures around the world, professional positions, programs like Project SEED and ACS (American Chemical Society) scholars and charitable society to fulfil his love and suffocation for chemistry. His visionary leadership is instrumental in furthering chemistry and ensuring continued opportunities in the field.

Fortune favors the brave and failure finds strength of success for winners. Like spectroscopy, sterochemistry is considered like a difficult subject before a Chemistry student. However, for a progressive pupil, quality is primary irrespective of its difficulty. To justify let us look into a story. One day a man came with questions from a very long distance to the king in the last minutes of the day set for hearing to his subjects. The king told the man to come in the next day because the day set was going to be almost over. However, the man expressed his tiredness of long journey and urgency of the solutions to the questions. The king then considered his prayer with condition that due to lapse of time he can ask only one but most difficult question. The man agreed and asked, "Which of egg or hen has come to this earth first" ? The king quickly said, egg and went away. The man was not convinced, hence questioned, "How" ? While going, the king made the man convinced by saying, "This is your second question".

As a great chemist of nineteenth century Emil Fischer has his contribution of Fischer's Projection for chiral compounds and Fischer's Proof for configuration of D-glucose. The lock and key relationship between enzyme and glucoside is a stereochemical link that must be set before putting chemical impact on each other. Emil Fischer is popular for elucidation of stereochemistry of carbohydrates. The problem of drawing three-dimensional configurations on a two-dimensional surface, such as a piece of paper, has been long standing concern of chemists. The wedge and hatched line notations we have been using are effective, but can be troublesome when applied to compounds having many chiral centres. As a part of his Nobel Prize-winning research on carbohydrates, he devised a simple notation called Fischer Projection drawing (formula) that is still widely used.

Streroselective synthesis of Pyrazofurin, a C-nucleoside has in fact given the author a lot of excitement to meet his suffocation for service in the fight between drug and disease while working as a Post Doctoral Associate (PDA) in the University of South Florida, Tampa, USA during late 1980s and early 1990s. To suffocate from shortage that could provide suffocation for surplus is virtually the strength to proceed. It is remarkable to observe the suffocation for work in the weak days bringing suffocation for entertainment in the weak end. The author feels pleased to observe the pleasure of suffocation for work any where in the laboratory or outside. Needless to say, great people are far ahead in this context. That is why we move. That is why we evolve in life.

* * * * *

Retro-synthesis, a Chess Game and Molecular Models

"Retrosynthetic Analysis" is a technique for solving problems in the planning of organic synthesis. This is achieved by transforming a target molecule into simpler precursor structures regardless of any potential reactivity with reagents. This procedure is repeated until simple or commercially available structures are reached. We have formalized this concept in our book, "The Logic of Chemical Synthesis".

Elias James Corey

A logical and more practical method for synthesizing molecules by working backward from the desired products with the visual aid of molecular models added a new dimension to complex molecule synthesis. Atoms and molecules are too small to be visible by human naked eye. Despite the large size of certain molecules like polymers of natural or synthetic origin, single molecules like haem, chlorophyll, vitamin B-12 and unimolecular micelle, the position and arrangement of atoms or groups in these molecules in space are not visible even by the help of electron microscope. However, electron cloud pictures of these, like the motion picture of the blades of a fast moving fan or an ignited match stick are observed. The cloud of water vapours is visible while individual water molecules are not. The Magnetic Resonance Imaging (MRI), the Scanning Tunneling Microscopy (STM) and (Cryo) Electron Microscopy are quite useful today for this purpose. X-ray and electron diffraction or even (cryo) electron microscopy techniques are not useful to biological system because they affect the living cells. Super Resolution Light Microscopy (SRLM) based on fluorescence is very much useful for molecular pictures in the living system.

Visual aid provides an additional way of understanding molecules better. Various compounds in space are, therefore, viewed through the artificially designed flexible models and accordingly their behavior in chemical environment is studied. Some of such models are the "Spring and Ball" model, the "Ball and Stick" model and the "Driding" model etc. Synthesizing a complex organic molecule is much like playing a game of Chess. Working backward from the desired molecule theoretically (retrosynthetically or antithetically), a chemist envisioned how it can be split into constituent parts (called synthons) and what could be the parent compounds (called synthetic equivalents) generating these synthons. This procedure is continued to get small simple synthesis of desired products. However, at each step of the processes the chemist is faced with more possible moves like a Grandmaster in a tournament play.

Fortunately, Chemistry has its grandmasters too, who have been instrumental in developing logical methods to help chemists find the wining line of play for synthesizing organic molecules. Quite a few chemists all over the world at present are striving hard to look for the basic principles underlying synthesis in order to develop logical coherent approach in forming complex organic molecules from simple precursors. The idea of working backward from their molecules is being taken as the beginning of the complex synthesis today. Elias James Corey, a pioneering chemist of Harvard University, USA in this field was the first to grasp the power of big pictures instead of trying to solve the problem. This enabled him to determine logically the best of each step of moves in the "Synthesis Chess" game. He has the ability to do "Total Synthesis, hitherto play impossible compounds according to simple logical principles."

And just computers have been taught play Chess, it has also been programmed the "Retrosynthetic Analysis" into computer. The use of artificial intelligence to help design a synthesis, has grown to a height that includes quite a lot of people today.

The strength of Dr. Korey's suffocation to find biomolecules in hand has in fact added a new dimension in molecular synthesis. The way of blocking all possible routes except one through which the journey of molecular synthesis is made to the target molecule, needs not only conceptual clarity on understanding the nature of molecular structure and function involved but also suffocation as a power of strength to move.

* * * * *

The Priest of Nature

A sustainable humane and benevolent philanthropic person !
If he stands it's like crowd and a single pillar can afford to high mansion.
Pioneered and made us stand !
All sudden it's a tearing twilight, he zeroed the breath.
Unbelievable ! Like a tidal current shock !
Mused with self esteem, nothing he expressed. Lived in own way.
Salute to the legend, salute His Rules !!
Never had we thought that night, a sight of grief and a sight of void.
No one can fill for god has made it's call of Nature !
But "KING IS KING no body would replace the spot.
Wish the divine soul unite ", with eternity and rest in peace !!

Mitrabhanu Dalbehera   Nityananda Biswal

So far known only earth is found to host living system. The ecological balance between plants and animals-the two inter dependent living systems is being slowly and steadily understood. We are indebted to science that it has established before us this inter dependence and sharing between plants and animals to sustain life. Animal takes oxygen (the gas released to air by plant) from air and converts carbohydrate (the food prepared by plant) to carbon dioxide and water with release of energy necessary for its own activities (**Respiration**). On the other hand plant takes carbon dioxide from air (the gas released to air by animal), water from soil and prepares carbohydrate (the food necessary for animal) in presence of sunlight (**Photosynthesis**). This beauty of Nature speaks of how plant and animal reciprocate each other for their simultaneous coexistence. As a lesson from Nature let us learn to share with each other for the development of not only the human race but the life itself. However, it is being affected with advancement of science in the material world and deterioration of ethics in the moral world. Man continues to enjoy the status of the most developed creature on earth. With use of its powerful brain and mind it wants to exploit Nature, care for only itself and therefore, loses conscience. By the way, man's quest and query to understand the secrets of Nature–the natural facts and figures, have made irreparable loss and damage to the environment and hence to himself knowingly or unknowingly through industrialization and merciless scientific innovation. This has now become an international issue which man has realized late and is concerned about. But unfortunately no unanimous global decision has yet come in any issue affecting everyone in general because of simply promoting one's own national interest of a country in particular before the interest of the entire human race and above all life itself. This needs improvement for the sake of Nature, life and humanity as a whole.

On the 31st day of December 1934, a baby came to the Biswal family of a very small and remote village, Gunthasahi with mostly ignorant and illiterate but simple people of Nayagarh district in Odisha of our country (India). The baby, in fact, came impregnated with great love for Nature, love for plants and animals, love for the role of plants and animal towards life, love for village life, love for education and love for simplicity and honesty in a complex living system like man. As the baby grew up to a boy then to a man he slowly realized and made many others feel the importance of education and environment for life. He tried his best to educate not only himself but his kith and kin, friends and relatives. He tried to activate the welfare of education and environment conducive for life till he breathed his last. He was a science teacher named Nityananda Biswal in a government high school. His passion for betterment of education and environment remained incomparable in the region. He took steps for his children not to lose even a single class in school. He wanted his men not to cut even a single tree. Moreover, he has spread the message of planting at least one tree in everybody's life. The effort that he has made to see his children educated has been witnessed by the river Kushumi between village and school while crossing it with two children on his shoulders at chest-height of water during rainy season. His long standing effort for a bridge to the village over this river from the government became successful to see the initiation only. However, it could not be completed during his life. Moreover, he was feeling happy to work on it for educational, economic and social development of the village because he knew that communication was primarily important for all round development of an area. His suffocation and strength paid him posthumous. The bridge was built up to connect the village with school, hospital, police station, etc. in the small town of Orgaon. The powerful message and makes that he has left will continuously keep education and environment elevated. Education builds career while environment builds the quality in life. The conceived Nature-loving quality became visible in his day to day activities. As a result, varieties of trees have been planted and cared in and around the village. He has proved himself as an ideal teacher in the region. A small pond of his own has been dug for the benefit of the villagers. The agriculture that he cultivated was a prime mean of self reliance for food and livelihood. These have certainly added both in principle and practice to the sustenance of quality life on earth, though in miniature, but has left massive message for the human race. The awareness that he has earned from his love for Nature is perhaps not achievable by education evaluated by qualification. He was educated enough to realize the importance of plants for healthy life on earth. The suffocation that he was feeling for the reign of rural life and restoration of ecological balance of Nature-his natural temple is respectable.

A number of relations remember and recite the joyous moments of his golden days of good deeds. The man is no more with us but has left his ideals that will certainly guide us in at least believing in the power of suffocation of his love for the above and the pleasure he received thereby. All on a sudden, that cruel day of fact came on January 11, 2014, took him away from all of us and left behind a void of sorrow and sufferings. However, no time has yet come and I am sure, will not come in future to snatch that what he has given, written in golden letters through his body, mind and heart. 'O' Noble Soul, let you be of us and let us continue to feel that we are of yours in the days to come.

Purna Pradhan (Son-in-law)

* * * * *

Young Man of Committed Work can not Die

> Jim Rohn was a very famous American author and entrepreneur. He was also one of the most widely known influential motivational public speakers. He was known for his inspiring speeches. The way he moved from bottom to top because of his hard work, dedication and determination is a source of inspiration for many others.
>
> Motivation is what gets you started. Commitment is what keeps you going.
>
> Jim Rohn

Unlike birth, the entry into and death, the exit from a body, melting and boiling points are two conditions of temperature and pressure finding solid-liquid and liquid-gas equilibria. Pre-matured death may be compared with volatilization of a solid. Irrespective of the phase whether solid or liquid or gas or anything else matter is somehow more recognized by its properties. Like phases are reflected in temperature and pressure, human quality is reflected in age, experience and activity. Life is so far mortal. It will continue to remain so unless and until some thing different comes to the mechanism of life. To have a possible change in the mechanism leading life to immortality, Sri Aurobindo has provided evidence in his "Savitri" and "Life Divine". Evolution will make the job possible. Simply speaking, so far no body is able to go to mars. This does not mean no body will be able to go to mars. Can we consider the nutrition necessary for life, hence body, mind, spirit or soul and their environment as certain factors responsible for sustaining life on earth ? If yes, then for evolution of life there could be changes in those. For an evolutionary change in life there would be suffocation from the existing one for an expected life with a suitable change in the mechanism.

With less knowledge and more faith on Sri Aurobindo philosophy, the author reached thirty years of his age. Back in 1988 when came to Rourkela to begin his professional career as a lecturer in Chemistry he found himself into a small community of people bound by a thread of spiritualism and love through Yoga Mandir, Roourkela, a place to feel for peace. Though the impact of involvement with small children could not be witnessed in Rourkela and in fact it was in Burla, he, however, became very happy to interact with a unique personality of vision for change towards betterment. Very common to look at, very different to look into, very sweet to speak, very fast to receive, very sensitive to touch and quite committed to work, the personality is Ashok bhai [Ashok Kumar Nayak, professionally a clerk in State Bank of India (SBI) but a spiritual leader in passion]. The author like iron, cobalt or nickel within no time became pulled to the magnetic moves of Ashok bhai in word and work as well. Both loved each other to go for a common target under the guidance of the Divine Mother. Bikram Keshari Mohanty (Nalu bhai), professionally an Engineer in Rourkela Steel Plant (RSP) but mentally a dare devil in Mother's work, became an inseparable part in the party of progressive work taken up by Yoga Mandir during late 1980s. Ashok bhai's suffocation off incomplete and insufficient work assigned to him has always provided the necessary strength and skill for quantitative and qualitative completion. In the march for immortality on earth shown by Sri Aurobindo and The Mother, Ashok bhai has dedicated himself to the tune of his total commitment. He used to move in the entire district of Sundargarh with a view to spreading the message of Sri Aurobindo and The Mother into the minds and deeds of as many people as possible. He gets immense strength to work beyond his professional hours committed to the SBI.

The author feels feared to stand before Ashok bhai to express as if he is a worker in Mother's motion and moves for evolution of life. This great feeling that Ashok bhai was carrying is still to come from the author who is however, grateful to his own brother (late Sankar Pradhan) to bring to the awareness of Supramental Consciousness when he was a boy of only five years. Slowly and steadily Mother's activities in Yoga Mandir went on with the pace of time to find continued attachment of the group with enthused Hitansu, Dama, Pankaj, Madhuchhanda, Guddy, Runu, Bina apa, Kenedy apa and many others besides Ashok bhai, Nalu bhai and the author himself. Needless to say the author is indebted to the spontaneous sensation of Ashok bhai to find a person like him. However, he is unfortunate not to even partly share with what Ashok bhai necessarily needed one day from him. It was too late to find him prepared for the need. He did not know that his Ashok bhai was nearing a cruel stroke of his fate.

The group was inspired to act with Kshyama apa and Shobha apa in Mother's deeds in and around Rourkela. It was to wonder and enjoy listening to Madhuchhanda narrating "Savitri" even at her teen age in "Pathachakra" in Yoga Mandir. The teenager was blessed with Divine Touch to carry on well not only in her professional Engineering but in personal passion. The author was lucky to work with her in this noble project of Sri Aurobindo and The Mother.

The author has heard people saying "Those whom God loves die young". Can a Young man turn old with age?

Can a committed work die ? The physical body of Ashok bhai left him and he went all on a sudden off this earthen world. His body was requiring necessary transformation to hold on life further. So, as per our Hindu Philosophy he had to look for a fresh body for continuation of his work. If we believe in rebirth, then nothing to be so unhappy in the present crisis but better to sustain the pain of his vital mishap and pray God for continuation of his Divine work and eternal peace. We are thankful to God that He has sent us with spiritual mind and belief in the evolution of mortal man to immortal Superman. So, let us continue to join hands without break in this noble work as Ashok bhai did till he breathed his last. Consequence will come automatic after work. So, it is better to leave it to Him and only work as an instrument. All along his life Ashok bhai has kept his cool to work both in principle or practice without caring whether slow or fast, more or less, small or big. So, let us hope that Fortune will favour his brave action and allow him rest in completion and peace.

Purna Pradhan (Purna Bhai)

* * * * *

A Noble Soul

Ways are many provided we sincerely want to do.	God is not present in idols. Your feelings are your God. The soul is your temple.
Suresh Pradhan	*Chanakya*

As per Hindu philosophy it is believed that at different times when vice overcomes virtue and crosses its limit in earth, God comes down in different form to reestablish justice and reload faith in god. So far ten different forms called 'Avtars' of God have been manifested in earth. As it appears in 'Kaliyug' today the normal go of human life is passing through a pseudo-spiritual phase. Falsehood and hypocrisy appear to surpass truth and reality. Mostly people rush to temples, mosques, churches or so either out of fear or for favour. Negligibly a few seek for God out of love, emotion and attachment. By mind, man runs for the immediate return of its every effort that to in cash. He does not understand in practice the objective of planting a tree today for the benefit of his successor tomorrow. This conceptual difference in ideal and actual purpose could be a cause of his sorrow and suffering of today.

Man continues to entertain mythological stories through reading, recitation, play, serial or cinema using updated technology in a very colourful manner as far as practicable. The covering of man's material attitude has become so thick and strong that he can not get out of it and hardly finds time and taste for moral thinking. So he does not get the flavor behind these stories of incidents in past. However, for a noble soul material activity necessary to run a life is not a blocking bar for noble thought and action. Impregnated with noble mentality a baby was born in a remote village about fifty years ago. He is the fourth and last child of his parents. Slowly with time he grew older after being affected by a series of diseases in turn till he completed sixteen years of his age. Academically he is a medium class student with fascination for science in general but automobile in particular. While reading commerce in intermediate level, he devoted his maximum time towards knowledge on automobile working rather than reading commerce. He, therefore, discontinued commerce study and admitted into Intermediate in Science (ISc). He passed ISc with average overall performance. He wanted to see the zoology department of the college equipped with specimen for demonstration to the students. As and when opportunity came he collected certain important sample specimen for the department. As a good foot ball player he has also earned fame during early hours of his college career. His inner will is to build up good relationship with its environment that he faces in his day to day life. He was too a good cyclist to his credit. He was, therefore, enjoying his daily thirty kilometer to and fro cycling between village and college besides holidays. He was very quick in cycling and was comfortable to ride up to 100 kilometers in a day.

At village he had a very good relationship with almost all villagers irrespective of caste and creed, young or old. He was having a strong suffocation for good relationship with as many people as possible beyond his village too. He is of an exemplary good relationship with his school teachers till their death. He has managed to keep almost frequent physical contact with them till date. He has been instrumental to bind the students of his batch of class 11 with possible financial and moral aid to socially weaker in the batch. This kind of his activities shows that he has a special passion for sharing pleasure of his own and pain of others. Of course he is not financially and socially very stable. Yet he claims to say " If we want to do ways are many". He enjoys his activities. So the author wanted him to give a unique recognition which is ordinarily not seen in society today.

Residing in a metropolitan city like Bhubaneswar, the epicenter of the state, Odisha, he has been pulling his family of wife, one daughter and one son aspiring for medical and engineering studies respectively. The hard work of meeting their requirements is very painful for him. His constant encouragement has made the children to run after their aim. In school level he has so far arranged innovative projects of his own idea related to automobile and his children have got the recognition and reward several times. As a father he has so far tried his best to support his children. As son his duty is exemplary. With a very low limited uncertain income it is quite struggling to run a family in a city like Bhubaneswar. Despite his poor income he is lucky to have kept his parents with him till their death. In the civilized society of today very few families like from inner core of heart to run with their old, weak, unhealthy, diseased, dependent parents of no income source at all. A few families may like to be with their old parents when the family is likely to be supported by the pension or any other source of direct or indirect income of parents. Some think and act to find their parents as liability instead of resource. It is a matter of regret to know that in some academic curriculum of preliminary education, concept of 'family' is confined to father, mother, son and daughter but there is no place of grand parents who necessarily need the hospitality and care of their kith and kin, most importantly their son or daughter. Despite his hard fought days he has made his dream fruitful to fly with his mother from Bhubaneswar to Kolkata for the sake of bringing the feeling of flying in a plane to his eighty years old mother. His suffocation to show his parents the various parts of Southern Odisha could not be made fruitful before their death. He, therefore, managed to fulfil his dream by touring all important visiting places of Southern Odisha with the photograph of his parents with a feeling as if they were with him.

As a noble personality he has been extending help and cooperation to near and far relations coming to him in Bhubaneswar for medical assistance and treatment. In arranging hospital/doctor he has experience as patient and access to many doctors of higher repute. He himself was a cancer patient and has undergone a major surgery in a prime hospital in Bhubaneswar followed by six chemotherapeutic doses. During this period of his own medical treatment he was strongly oriented for Yoga in principle and practice. His dedication for Yoga has not only help saved from a lethal disease like cancer but recognized him as a true practitioner of Yoga in body, mind and heart both as a student and a teacher. It is hard to believe to earn span for life tomorrow by cutting down the earning necessary for today and finding time for Yoga. To his knowledge human is a complex system of body, mind sprit, psyche and soul. Yoga is a way to take care of all of these. In spite of all his financial hardship and acute shortage of time he has never denied any body to find time and interest for possible help within the purview of his limits. As a human he finds a great pleasure in it. He really suffocates and is committed to this kind of job beyond his only way of earning and sustaining his family. His suffocation is in fact providing certain strength to continue his way of working shown so far.

He is never frustrated and harassed to run his family even in period of crisis. His spiritual belief and courage to face the obstacle have saved him so far. Both as an automobile (non-living car) driving trainer and as a human system (living car) driving yoga teacher he teaches his students with principle, practice and undeterred faith necessary in driving. He too suffocates for innovative ways to train out of his internal call. His is a unique and successful training not only to his wish and aspiration but to his only way of earning for his family. He feels, his suffocation has paid him strength and span to move with his family till date though not quite comfortably yet manageably. As a well wisher and supporter of his moves the author salutes this noble soul and prays God to bliss him healthy mind and healthy body so that he would continue to suffocate for his unique work and derive pleasure and peace in the days to come.

Purna Pradhan (Brother)

* * * * *

An Appeal to the CM

God, our Creator has stored within our minds and personalities, great potential strength and ability. Prayer helps us tap and develop these powers.

A. P. J. Abdul Kalam

God speaks in the silence of the heart. Listening is the beginning of prayer.

Mother Teresa

We continue to believe that health is wealth and education, a subtle part of health is inevitable. Still some people do not hesitate to say that departments of health and education are departments of loss and are unproductive. Of course this feeling in mind brings a lot of loss in building a man where education has an important role. Further, teaching is a noble job. Teachers are the workers in man making industry. The quality that upgrades a man to human is humanity. Government is outsourcing a lot of funds taking care for teaching, teacher and taught so that quality education can reach every individual human. In spite of all efforts, the level of education does not find an elevation as per expectation to compare with national and international standard. Most people in teaching are not inclined for teaching. Too many children do not come to school or leave school early. A few manage to go overseas for higher study. Of them very few almost negligible return from abroad after higher study and settle for service of mother land, but instead stay back even in a much less dignified manner. We are now almost extinct in national or international ranking concept of education in terms of university/research institute to come within even top 100. Our name does not find a place in the Nobel list of science subjects like Physics, Chemistry and Physiology or Medicine for too many years. Where could be some certain lapses for these irregularities ? The author has been suffocating from such irregularities for he has been suffocating for a very healthy education system in the state.

To the author, education is a passion of the student, teacher and the people behind. Our ancient education was culturally very strong. In contrast, our modern education is far behind both academically and culturally as well. In fact, elevation of education does not happen overnight. It is a long and hard fought consequence. It is not one man's job but a team effort. Quite a good number of nations have managed to establish top quality education in their countries before us in modern days. Can we not learn from these ?

Our educational output has gone down much below national and international standard. Our educational input is also not so attractive. Our educational interest is not at all sufficient. We do not find quality teachers. We do not find quality teaching. We do not have quality educational institutions too. Above all we do not have mind setup for quality education in the state. What the author feels, we do not find adequate necessity, interest, inspiration and aspiration for study among students, teaching among teachers and suitable environment of governance in the administration in the true spirit of mind and heart. Above all we do not find someone specific who can think and feel and do a lot for a developed system of education and give top priority to it. There is difference among the views - to do something, the purpose behind doing something and path in which the deed is done for a particular purpose. All of these must be analyzed carefully before evaluating educational output. Perhaps our purpose, objective or attitude and path are not rich enough for a healthy education in the state. Ways are many to look for the betterment of student, teacher and teaching. The most important of all these is the way of openness with love and dedication for education. Any body in the name of teacher in a class of students is not necessarily a teacher. Something spoken by a teacher in the name of teaching in a class of students is not necessarily teaching. Anybody listening in a class to a teacher is not necessarily a student. Moreover, student, teacher and teaching are defined. They must maintain their descent standard throughout. Student must be complementary to teaching and teacher. Teaching must be compatible to the teacher. And above all, the teacher must be fit for imparting education. Student, teacher and teaching must be proportionally good to reciprocate one another. Overall, the right work in right path must be maintained.

It is a matter of regret to observe that education now in private/public sector is being increasingly considered as a profit making concern like business. Education is being industrialized as an income source. The main objective is material gain not quality education. In fact the real profit that the nation is investing for is being forgotten. People in power exploit educational organizations in private, public or even government sectors for their hard or soft gains in the name of assistance. Education in the institution is being disturbed in a variety of ways. Minimum educational aid is a plea but the real interest is something different what is not at all encouraging for education. Concentration is focused on uneducated illiterate poor people who can be purchased directly or indirectly. Again, attention is away from qualified and somehow educated mass as if they are not reliable. Further, mostly academic ideals are followed but not implemented. People involved from top to bottom contribute in miniature to the deterioration of education in the state. In educational institutions mostly teaching is conducive to non-teaching teachers. In academics, works like admission, administration, examination, evaluation, promotion, office management etc. are somehow being managed, however, without quality teaching and performance. Work culture is deteriorated. Teaching faculties are more inclined towards co-curricular activities but decline to go for curricular activity like teaching, the primary assignment. The situation in real/fundamental research is discouraging. Moreover, backlog of non-teaching works in teaching institution makes the teachers less or not available for teaching. The most difficult and unwilling job in academic institution is teaching. In addition, research in undergraduate institutions is discouraging in spite of official notice from the government. Mere notice is not enough. Infrastructural arrangement and suffocating bent of mind are necessary to be inculcated for research. The out come of education and research that we observe today is obvious because of almost no reward or no punishment if someone does or does not go for teaching/research. The corruption and exploitation in government machinery to delay or deny the dues to the deserving could be a major reason for the poor educational status of the state. People in education suffer like anything for their post retirement benefit after superannuation. Even for years after retirement in the government sector many are being victimized as prey by the predator of poor machinery management not to have their deserving dues. People are running from pillar to post with hesitation and hatred for the management of such a noble profession to get their age old necessity at the old age. It is a matter of regret to know that the UGC has no hold on state government to implement UGC norms in toto on the state government teachers under UGC fold when the former contributes 80 % of finance required. Variety of teaching faculties like temporary teacher, contractual teachers, sikshya sahayak, sikshya karmi, guest faculty, etc. with large differences in their payment in forms of salary or aid are being introduced for the same education. There is no permanent and concrete provision to eliminate this kind of discrimination. Besides quality, quantitatively the number of faculties is much less than the required. The difference in the age of superannuation is again a cause of concern. After continuous service of more than twenty years a state government employee in education sector does find the post retirement benefit like pension after 2005 whereas an MLA enjoys the same benefit after serving even for a day. With so much of difference in practice and principle in the input in quality, quantity and consideration, the result we find today is quite reasonable. There is nothing like astonishing in it. If we look into the education in the western developed world and the attitude in general for education there, we must feel guilty. Exceptions are very few and therefore, never examples. Who is responsible for the educational injury of our teacher, taught or teaching ? Is it time ? Is it the temperament ? Is it education policy ? Is it the policy maker ? Is it the mode of implementation of the policy ? Is it the person by which the policy is implemented ? Or is it the spectrum of all of these ? Time is overdue to think and act on these questions.

It is unfortunate to take any people with minimum requirement for teaching as teacher in different names without any/proper selection and consider them as senior on the basis of date of joining compared to those who have joined as teacher after being selected through proper procedure. Strength of unity, number and early born/entry to the job is exploited to go out of the way so that the genuine and deserving is neglected. It is unfortunate again to express that the educational level can be pushed to a lower minimum by keeping eyes on the benefit to a very few undue people in a shrewd manner. Government machinery is often misused to find undeserving in the position. Social enemies like corruption, canvassing, bribery etc. are not removed from academic spheres. As a result the academic environment is not only degraded but gets over crowded with the misdeeds of the undeserving, once placed in a position. Very few academicians with interest in education and research, entered into educational institutions do not feel free, fair and favoured for academic excellence. An example is cited here. A man at the age of 60 after superannuation is now in uncertainty of repentance as if he has committed a mistake by opting research as his career after completion of M.Sc. degree in 1982 instead of joining as a lecturer at least in a private college which were large in number and easy to enter into. Had he been at least a private college lecturer which was quite possible in 1983 instead of entering into research which he considered a potentially stronger and better step, he would have retired today as a senior UGC reader with a salary of about 1.8 lakhs per month and pension of about 0.9 lakh per month what is being found in case of his contemporary mates (without even a single degree of higher study beyond master's) who preferred lectureship in a private college with the then salary of less than 500 rupees per month, instead of research. However, on the other hand this man with successful M.Phil. (1984), NET (1985), Ph.D

(1988) (through CSIR research fellow) and Post Doctoral Associate (PDA)(1989-91) in a much developed country like USA and much developed field like synthetic nucleosides and nucleotides as drug. Unfortunately, this man has taken his retirement on superannuation as a mere state scale reader after much humiliated phases of entry into and exit from the government system. In terms of financial gain it is a matter of pain and shame to look at self in presence of UGC readers of the state and discouraging not to find even a few of such cases. So, question comes from the core, 'who and what are responsible for these' ? This kind of difference has terrible impact on not only the life of an individual directly but the educational fate of a state indirectly and is no doubt a clear example of harassment for higher education and research. The little but great interest - the love for mother land dragged the man from the then attractive incentives of western developed world to the miseries of long continuing underdeveloped eastern land. The way he had thought to serve his mother land did not happen. The most of the ongoing procedures and practices were too difficult for him to follow either in principle or in practice.

Two refresher courses, twenty one days of duration each, have in fact found more important and therefore, given more weight than Ph.D degree for consideration of promotion. Most teachers like, accept and adopt the policy of 'first come first serve' irrespective of mode of entry to the job and academic achievements. The teachers are not ready to face any kind of test/assessment as eligibility for special incentive. Rather they focus on the date of joining as the only criterion. Therefore, they reacted in wrath with explosion in early 1990s to oppose a proposal of a special test as eligibility for a special incentive like UGC scale. This is not fair for education in the state. The consequence of this unfortunate attitude of the teachers is in the front now. On the other hand there is no clear cut policy in the state. Implementation of UGC scale is confined to a particular group of people on the basis of joining in the service in a particular time period irrespective of academic credential. The unfair binding of refresher courses for promotion under UGC scale is a humiliation not to consider the degrees like M.Phil, Ph.D, NET or even higher. It is again unfair to waive such binding for promotion in certain cases under special ground different from M.Phil, Ph.D, NET or so. Rome was not built in a day. Likewise, education does not deteriorate in a day. Unless it is watched and cared properly, very soon it would go to hell.

Developed countries like Japan, Germany, the US etc. may be followed by each individual involved in education. Most importantly, the heads of state and government are to be vigilant to take care of all these aspects of education- the way for life quality. Both teaching and research are dedications to the nation. Then, who is there to take care of the teachers ? Now, let us imagine the fate of such teachers and researchers. Can we survive without teaching/ research, i.e., education ? Can we survive with teaching/ research unless the teachers/researchers are adequately looked after ? Most experienced academicians have a common feeling of the drainage of young minds after Information Technology instead of Basic Education and after western attraction instead of serving own mother land even for a day. The reasons are more or less known. What the author feels to appeal, <u>" Let there be positive attitude with priority that educational update is essential for all round improvement of the state. Let there be free and fair avenues for selecting persons fit to teach/carry out research both by talent and temperament. Let there be real execution of periodic assessment followed by suitable action (reward/</u>

punishment). Let there be offer of substantial pay and perk and most crucially let there be feeling of what we use to recite from our culture,

Guru Brahma Guru Bishnu Gurudev Maheswarah,
Guru Sakshyat Param Bramha Tasmai Sri Gurave Namah,

so that these two vital instruments of quality life will not only be honoured but the state will flourish spontaneously.

It is good to remember that a similar feeling has been communicated in 2009 to the Chief Minister of the sate and an appeal is made for all round development of education in the state with copy to heads of premier departments, viz. Development Commissioner, Commission-cum-Secretary, Special Secretary and Director of Higher Education. When this kind of feeling is extended to the citizens who would suffocate from the constraints and for suitable changes towards healthy growth of education, there would be established a different but developed era of education in the state and the citizens would cross the limits of their own education bound by qualifications. Basically suffocation would bring the inspirational energy for progressive and constructive steps for the much needed education in everybody's life.

* * * * *

Superannuation - A Transition in Life

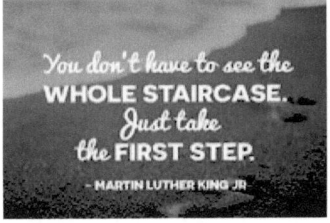 

Evolution is inevitable. Knowingly or unknowingly it goes on. With internal will and external environment it becomes slower or faster. It is a spontaneous process both in living and non-living matter. Though the exact mechanism is not known and theory is yet to be established, it appears as if life has evolved from lifeless. Because of evolution we the human beings are here. Think of a non-living system in the level of a molecule called reactant in a chemical reaction. When a reactant remains in stress or strain under a particular set of conditions what we call environment, it may change to a suitable product with a rate that is directly proportional to the stress or strain that the reactant suffers from and the stability of the product that it enjoys. Since the important components of a reaction are the reactant, the product and the reaction condition—the environment, chemical reactions can be controlled kinetically by activation energy of the reactant and thermodynamically by potential energy of the product. When we plot a graph between a particular parameter of a system versus time, it becomes curvilinear because of several ups and downs.

However, the overall change of the system is positive and progressive in Nature's deed.

Retirement on superannuation snatches something from a life but offers something else so that the net is favorable. For this reason, life evolves. Socrates before his death said to his followers, "We don't know yet whether that side is better or this side. Let us hope we are moving towards betterment". For a growing species it does not mind what environment it faces. Its inherent will, work and ambition take the opposing environment in the path as positive and catalyst. So, it enhances its zeal and vigor. Quite often we fail to accept this truth. So, we start blaming the environment and time. But we should not forget that while doing so, only one finger is towards the environment or so and the rest four are towards us.

As senior, experienced and matured man, we have a lot to do for the family, the society, the nation, the human race and above all the life on earth which are at the verge of being fragile and endangered. There is a conflict between matter and morale. Day by day the average life is tempted towards easy but wrong goings. For his effort man wants the return immediately that to in cash. Short term temporary benefit drives down the right path. The 'should' and 'should not' are least cared. The risk and danger are not seen. The suffocation for global power has no limit. The use of detonators and nuclear energy has in fact lost direction to save life. The reasons for these in the journey of mind are not known by the author, a little creature of God. Material science spreads without conscience to deal with Nature. Thanks to God, the pro-endangered life on earth is being slowly and steadily realized by human community. National and global bodies are mobilizing this awareness that unless we take immediate and adequate steps, this beautiful, compact and complex living system on earth may be endangered and extinct one day. Green technology as a bit of conscience appears to be introduced in the path of scientific efforts and achievements. Education and health- the two jewels of life, however, need a lot of healthy changes in the world in general but India in particular so that the ethical mind is evolved appreciably to adopt without delay. Both the maker and the made should come up jointly to give a concrete shape to this realization. Global leaders from all walks of life should stand on a common plat form of life which is at stake today. As an individual we should learn from the teaching of the squirrel in binding Ramsetu of the Ramayan, role of Mahatma Gandhi in setting India free from British brazen claws and many others. The past powerful cultural heritage of our country should be rebuilt in practice so that a green India leading to a green world would come out.

After 60, a considerable span of life, one is matured and moulded after being sunk or drowned into many different types of water and suffocated for many different types of oxygen. Man should realize the existence of God. If possible one may try for an equation connecting matter with spirit like the famous equation, $E=mc^2$ for theory (general or special) of relativity of Albert Einstein, the great. With vast experience and understanding one should continue this journey of work as an instrument under His command and control till **this end** that we know and **that beginning** which we don't. The ethical bent of mind should emerge now if not so far, so that the more we would move, closer we would be towards His touch and better we would feel to see the rising sun of tomorrow after the end of tonight.

* * * * *

Suffocation a Case Study

Suffocation from necessity may cause suffocation for invention or discovery which would bring inspiration of strength required to keep one alive in the race. Obstacle is an opportunity to be tested. Unless we fall we can not stand, unless we sink we can not learn swimming. Unless we are tested we can not justify.

Purna Pradhan (Author)

Atoms are stable. Molecules are more stable than atoms. When stability is disturbed, the species becomes reactive. This reactivity is a measure of instability. Irrespective of the fact that the species is living or non-living, it may or may not undergo change to a different species depending on the extent of suffocation, the instability, the excitation and hence the essential inspiration for the change. Suffocation is a soft, subtle change in the internal organ of an individual. It will suffocate or not, to more or less, depends on itself and its environment as well. Therefore, changes could be spontaneous or non-spontaneous. The former is somehow easy while the latter could be made spontaneous by adequate and appropriate external effort. For example, water can flow down spontaneously. However, it can go up with extra effort called work. Hydrogen mixes comfortably with oxygen to stay as a mixture. But once this mixture is ignited, explosive formation of water occurs.

We have to realize that excitement is necessary to proceed in life. Extra effort like work can bring success that spontaneously does not happen. Progress and its speed come out of the inconvenience with the present, the expected comfort from the future and the path in between. Suffocation provides proportionate energy for the change. A baby of less than a year falls so many times before being able to walk. A child faces so many hurdles before being able to run. A sprinter loses many a times before being winner. The impregnated and inherent will is responsible quantitatively and qualitatively for forward move. At the age of five a rural boy saw him in a nearby school more comfortable than at home. He felt more enthused and dynamic at school. Later he came across spiritual touch with Sri Aurobindo philosophy that man can evolve to superman a day. His elder brother was leading with this philosophy in the family. Since he was from a lower middle class family, study and then a job were both necessary for the family. He was no doubt studious with love for study. In class 1 to 5, he came out first in elementary education because anything less provided him necessary suffocation for so. In class 6 to 11, however, it was not enough to maintain the position but sufficient for the next. He is more than obliged to his science teachers, Sri. Purna Chandra Pradhan and Sri Prafulla Chandra Dash in class 6 to 11 for sowing the seed of science interest in his fertile mind. Sri Sachidananda Mishra, head master taught English grammar in his unique style with emphasis on English as an international medium for communication.

Sri Purna Chandra Pradhan
Science Teacher, High School

(Late) Basudev Dash
English Teacher,
High School

Sri Sachidananda Mishra
Head Master, High School

Sri Prafulla Chandra Dash
Science Teacher,
High School

Sri Madan M Dash Odia
Teacher, M.E. School

Plate 1 : With five teachers who are used to pull the author into action both inside and outside the class room

The young boy now continues to inculcate scientific temper in the early hours of college education in 1976 for which he had to bike 15 kilometers to and fro daily. Before his zeal and vigor the physical pain of cycling from village to college and back every day remained undermined. He had made the provision of entry to the first class of the day irrespective of punishment in case of occasional delay that normally did not happen. During I.Sc., he preferred to sit in a seat away from direct view of the teacher with a purpose of showing something different but positive and unexpected response when asked by the teacher. Sri Daitary Behera, teaching inorganic chemistry and Sri A. V. P. R. Rao teaching physical chemistry are his inspirations to feel more about chemistry. However, the reason for the then special interest of the young boy in Organic Chemistry classes even though the mode of teaching was not so attractive, is not known even today. Perhaps it was the relation of the branch with living system and the boy was having a strong desire to enter into. He was feeling like without oxygen at home when found no class for a span of six weeks because of an accident leading to broken both hand injury. The accident of falling from a height of more than 30 feet while plucking black berry in a tree was enough to take his life. This did not happen because he is meant for some thing special to happen from a rural village of that time. The treatment in the nearby Subsidiary Health Centre (SHC) is unbelievable. On arrival with injury after accident it was found that there was no doctor, no compounder, no plaster of parish available for examination and necessary bandage. He had to wait in the veranda till his village mate returned with required materials for bandage from a nearby locality 8 kilometers away. Fortunately, Dasha bhaina, the behera (attendant) of SHC later supported by compounder took all the effort of risk and pain to set the hands into position and made the bandage manually and mechanically out of their experience only without X-ray. The boy carries the evidence of this work of 1976 in his bent hands even today as a mark of memory.

Plate 2 : Prof. Satyaban Jena, Chemistry Teacher (B.Sc), who is an inspiration of a lot of memory and talent in academics and non-academic life

Govind Samal
Classmate, B.Sc, M.Sc

Sangeeta Pani (Tiklu),
Classmate, B.Sc and M.Sc

Plate 3 : Two friends, remembered to have shared with the author since graduation (B.Sc) till today

On entering to his graduation in 1978 in G. M. College (now G. M. University), Sambalpur, the problem of regional feeling towards admission had terrified the spirited boy. Original documents were being snatched and torn off, once got exposed because of his eastern origin in the then Orissa (now Odisha). The boy hailed from Puri district of coastal belt about 450 kilometers away from Sambalpur and for this reason he was likely to fall into prey of some local boys of narrow regional feeling. Sri. C. M. P. Rao, lecturer in Physics helped him a lot to get admitted into B.Sc. course there without verifying original documents in spot. He managed to do it secretly with photo copies on the spot and original documents much later when the admission work was over and the situation came normal. Having more marks in Physics in I.Sc and getting selected into Chemistry honours, without much experience the boy could smell the role of Chemistry in living system as a matter of internal will and interest instead of that of Physics though that there is a branch called Biophysics. With running of college and class the boy continued to come by bus from Burla, a small town but educational nerve of the state, about 20 kilometers away from Sambalpur city. In the bus the ragging by local boys out of mean mental attitude was embarrassing to test that he was of some extra interest for study. Slowly, however, it went diminished from his path with time and the boy could become though not a friend but not also a foe to them.

With a lot of enthusiasm and emotion he was sitting by his mate Govinda, a student of passion, poverty and potential. He felt pleased all along to be associated with him as a friend both in academics and non-academics as well. He was glad to know that Govinda has passed B.Sc with First class, 2nd rank in Chemistry honours and distinction in Physics and Mathematics. Mrs. Manju Patnaik, a newly recruited lecturer was to take our first honours class. In response to her question on the number of elements discovered till date, most of the students answered 103 ending with element Lawrencium of atomic number 103. However, the boy was different to reply 105. Suddenly a burst of laughs echoed the room. "Have you discovered the rest two" ?

Dr. B.K.Mishra
RA (Later Professor),
Co-Guide (M.Phil, Ph.D)

Prof. R. K. Behera
Teacher,
(M.Sc and M.Phil)

Plate 4 : Two professors, friend and philosopher for the author in professional and private life as well

Prof. A. Nayak
Teacher and Guide (M.Sc)

Prof. G. B. Behera
Teacher and Guide
(M.Phil, Ph.D)

Plate 5 : Most lovable teachers for academic excellence and vision with power to drag towards self.

No", he replied gently to his mates. He was a regular reader of "Science Reporter" the subsidized monthly science magazine released by government of India even today. He was aware of the two discoveries, Kurchatovium (symbol Ku, atomic number 104, later adopted as Rutherfordium, symbol R_f) and Hahnium (symbol Ha, atomic number 105, later adopted as Dubnium, symbol Db) from this magazine just a few days ago. Most interestingly madam Patnaik questioned, can you say all the 105 elements now ? He to his credit could say all of these from Hydrogen-1 to the then Hahnium-105 in a single stroke, of course group wise. In fact this was the test of his tough task of remembering all the elements as a newcomer to chemistry honours. The chapter, however, was not ended there. Its after-effect started calling him Kurchatovium in the very next day by his fellow mates and he responded with a smile. That recognition works occasionally today by some, Ticklu in particular. His two years effort was reflected in the final examination result where he came out successful with first class Chemistry honours and distinction in Physics and Mathematics.

The love for chemical origin and chemical basis of life led him later in 1980 to M. Sc. programme in Sambalpur University in Burla itself with Organic Synthesis and Biochemistry as special paper. He was very much impressed by Prof. G. B. Behera and Prof. Ashutosh Nayak through their theoretical command and practical skill on the subject of Physical Organic Chemistry and Synthetic Organic Chemistry, respectively. All his attention during this period was concentrated on how to attract these two professors through response and result so that he will get an opportunity to work under their direct guidance from a very close proximity. Luckily he was selected for special paper in Organic Chemistry (synthesis of Purine and Pyrimidine analogs) under Prof. Nayak. He was more than happy, therefore, could not but met and asked Prof. Nayak when to start the special work. Slowly and steadily Prof. Nayak liked the boy to his satisfaction. The boy tried his level best to extract the experience and expertise from Prof. Nayak and was motivated to this branch of science much more than before. He loved Organic Chemistry so much that in an examination unfortunately he scored much less than what would have given him some comfort. He, therefore, quickly reacted and appeared the improvement- the provision of enhancement of performance without losing a year. This is because **he did not want to see such poor mark in his certificate**. He then came out successful in the improvement examination in the same year with excellent mark. The hunger and special affinity for organic chemistry of biological base later oriented him to work on synthesis of thiobarbituric acid derivatives as potential drug in his M.Phil program in the same chemistry department of Sambalpur University under the guidance of much awaited Prof. G. B. Behera, a stalwart in Physical Organic and Synthetic Organic Chemistry. Later he joined in a CSIR research project as Junior Research Fellow under Prof. Behera and then qualified National Educational Test (NET) in chemistry conducted by the University Grants Commission (UGC). He enjoyed research there to work even overnight. He was specially inclined to the organic environment of odour carrying both flavor and smell as identity in the laboratory. Dr. Bijay Kumar Mishra, the then research assistant and later professor in the same department, was nicely bridging the progress of the aspired boy with Prof. Behera. The research group of Prof. Behera including co-scholars namely Bramhamayee Sarangi, Pramila Kumari Mishra, Abhay Kumar Sahay, Sushree Senapati and few other teacher fellows like Lingaraj Nayak, Prabhat Kumar Das and Alaka Das and some M.Phil and P.G. students including K. P. Satpathy was with intimate cooperation of that of Prof. Nayak as if two wings of the same bird. The boy was very nicely collaborating with some members of research groups in the department of Life Sciences of same university because of his interest in the chemistry of living system. Sunakar Panda, chemistry student of Prof. Nayak, and Ph.D. scholar of Prof. U. C. Biswal of Life Sciences department was very much eager to connect Life Science with Chemistry in each pace of his work. Anuradha Patnaik and Hare Krishna Patnaik were among the biology friends to connect with chemistry ones beautifully. Prior to start with Prof. Behera in the Ph.D programme the boy was called by Dr. Pramod Chandra Mishra, another professor of Life Sciences department to work in a Biochemistry research project of UGC as a Ph.D. scholar under his guidance. However, the boy was innocent enough to continue to increase IQ and EQ in heterocyclic synthesis of purine and pyrimidine derivatives as drug. This was really interesting to enjoy. The graph of pleasure, peace and enjoyment of the boy in this period of mid 1980s with time continued to find positive slope.

Plate 6 : Author among a team of committed people in the laboratory. Back (L to R) : Ph.D Scholars-Sushree Senapati , Pramila Mishra, Purna Pradhan (author), Teacher-Dr. B. K. Mishra and Ph.D Scholar-Abhay Sahay Front (L to R) : Teacher Fellows-Mukesh Rawal, Lingaraj Nayak, Guide-Prof. G. B. Behera, Teacher-Dr. B. K. Sinha and Teacher Fellow-Ram Patnaik

Ph.D student, Abhay Sahay in action

Classmate (M.Sc) Kali Satpathy,

Plate 7 : Two feathers (like the author) of the same bird always ready to help the bird flying

It is of worth to remember one occasion in the laboratory when Prof. Behera called upon a post graduate student and sent her to bring a filtration flask. She came inside the laboratory where the boy was working undisturbed, moved in the laboratory throughout but did not find the flask because she could not really recognize a filtration flask. The boy intervened after a while and provided the flask she wanted. When Prof. Behera could know the incidence he asked her, "Who gave you the flask"? She told that someone present in laboratory gave me it. Someone, questioned Prof. Behera who got annoyed with her to tell, "You are working in the same research group and do not know each other. This should not happen in future." In fact, Prof. Behera as a very good research pioneer never liked to spare team spirit and mutual sharing in the group. He had the command to take the class for hours. While taking a class, for a small disturbance what he did not like he had to drive a student out with a message of anger not to show the face for fifteen days. The boy was silently observing Prof. Behera's wrath and his love for silent but stormy teaching. The boy was hardly staying in the hostel beyond lunch and dinner breaks. It was one day necessary to observe a reaction throughout. The boy was returning from laboratory to hostel at about 4 am in the morning. He was bit scared in dark to listen some sound from the turning nearby central library and then saw three ladies passing towards him. However, one of them, Anuradha Patnaik, a scholar of Life Sciences department could trace the boy from the horrible sound of his bike and basket and even more precisely the time of his return to hostel. Ms. Patnaik, a friend of the boy was to make her mind that this was the time when he returns to hostel very often. She with her two friends was moving very early in the morning to the nearby Hirakud railway station to catch the train to Rourkela, the place of her parents.

Plate 8 : Prof. B. C. Kar, V.S.S. Medical College, Burla [Guide in Sickle Cell Research Centre (SCRC)], Mrs. Surjeant, Dr. G. R. Surjeant, Jamaican Professor and Sri B. P. Dash, RA (like the author) (later Professor)
(From left to right)

In addition to research the boy was having fascination for drawing and painting. One day a task of drawing and painting of Goddess Saraswati in a wall in the department in the previous day evening was assigned to him to complete before 8 am next day. The suffocation for this work immediately made him prepared to start with less than 12 hours of night time in hand. He had to work all along and gave the finishing touch before 30 minutes of the scheduled. In a different occasion the department was organizing an international seminar, "Reaction on Micellar and Membrane Surface (ROMAMS)" with Japanese professor, Dr Haya Kawa as key note speaker. The boy was keenly involved in it and unfortunately fell sick of typhoid and could not attend the seminar. He was feeling in the hospital bed the touch of each and every progress of the seminar in the department. With tear in eyes he was thinking when someone is involved physically, mentally and emotionally how was it possible to keep him aloof from real execution of the preparation made before. This was not fair or there could be some lapse with himself. So he would have to work on it.

It could be worthy to mention here that one can learn the suffocation of Prof. Bikram Keshari Senapati who has started research on earth worm from grass root level in the department of Life Sciences. Prof. Senapati was very familiar with the boy and ever ready to inspire from his heart and mind. The timely support and moral boost that he had provided, the boy can never forget. With all kinds of support from both the departments in the case of the boy it became easy to climb up the steps of his mission even if the entire ladder was not visible. With Sri Aurobindo and The Mother philosophy on evolution of life from man to superman, Prof. Senapati had a lot of courage and confidence that the boy has shared with. The boy had to agree with Prof. Senapati that laboratory confined to four walls is not the only place to carry out research for which in fact there is no particular place or time. He emphasized on the fact that in the limitless natural field, Nature the scientist of scientists was doing research to leave many observations might be perceived by human being. The task is to receive these and give a concrete concept through the always open sensory organs, a much developed brain and a powerful evolving human system with mind and soul. In Sambalpur University the boy was then well set with his Ph.D degree in "Studies on Heterocyclic Compounds" under the guidance Prof. Behera to proceed for the next.

In the interest of the boy another feather was added to his crown of achievements when he got a chance to work with Dr B. C. Kar, a professor of Medicine in V.S.S. Medical College and Hospital, Burla in an I.C.M.R. research project on sickle cell anemia disease. Prof. Kar used to lead the team with his vast experience and expertise for survey, blood sample collection from localities of about 30 km radius from the Sickle Cell Research Centre (SCRC) of the college and conduct of certain tests with the collected blood followed by suitable socio-medical advice towards control and care of the disease. The boy was used to look after faetal haemoglobin estimation and other chemical analysis and interpretations while Dr Bishnu Prasad Dash, later professor in F. M. University, Balasore was taking care of electrophoresis and other biochemical analysis and involvements. Dr Dash hailed from the same village was very positive and inspired with the boy to extend his emotional work with the team. Jamaican professor, Dr G. R. Surjeant with his deep insight in the field was making catalytic visits to the centre to boost the morale of Prof. Kar and his team. The work was enjoyed with both pleasure and pain to collect blood sample from the area under survey. It was a daunting task to convince and collect sample against unwillingness out of illiteracy and ignorance and counsel to avoid trait-trait or trait-patient or patient-patient marriage. However, with a hope that fortune would favor the brave, the team was in its mission in full swing with a lot of suffocation, sacrifice and service to save certain society of Western Orissa (now Odisha) prone to the disease. The culture of work with the team is memorable.

Teaching is a noble job. The boy entered into it as lecturer in chemistry in Municipal College, Rourkela, an institution of its unique recognition in the entire state of the then Orissa (now Odisha). Both teacher and taught communities were to celebrate their dignity for years since inception in 1978. The dream of the boy for teaching and research stepped into practice in phases of research and teaching in turn. His dream for higher research overseas did not allow him quite often to sleep. His parents were not prepared enough to liberate him to cherish his desire of research in the western world. In 13th November 1989 he flew over Europe and Atlantic from Bhubaneswar through Delhi, Frankfort and New York to Tampa, Florida, U.S.A. The transition of applying came calm in university of South Florida to see him as an emerging post doctoral associate for a research project on synthetic nucleosides and nucleotides as drug funded by the U.S army and NIH with Prof. Stewart W. Schneller as Principal Investigator.

Prof Schneller triggered the energy of the boy by giving compete liberty to work at will whether in day or at night, to go for potential proposal and hence supporting chemicals to reach 100 mg of the target molecule. However, from safety and rescue view point he did not forget to caution the boy not to work alone in the laboratory. This speaks of responsibility and love as well of Prof. Schneller. Such full fledge freedom to flow fully with research the boy had never had before. So it was a special period that he continued to enjoy the entire two years of stay there with Professor Schneller, a scientist of talent, temperament and skill in synthetic biochemistry. He was eagerly waiting for the normal half an hour in every fifteen days scheduled visit of Prof. Schneller to discuss and comment on the progress. Moreover, Prof. Schneller had left option open for additional visit with prior appointment in case of exigency.

Plate 8 : Prof. Stewart W. Schneller (Guide), University of South Florida, Tampa, Florida, Guide, PDA (USA)

Plate 9 : Author (R) with Dr. Suhaib Siddiqi (L) and Dr. Wendlin Frick (M), Fellow PDAs in the US laboratory, the place and period for independent research in the career of the author

In non-academic private life Prof Schneller was not only friendly but a bit romantic too to his team members. In an occasion he invited the boy to his residence for a dinner. The boy responded with a rose bud in hand to professor himself. While offering he signaled the boy to do so to his wife, Jessica who he thinks is the right person to receive it, instead. Sometimes in week end in Tampa Atlantic beach, Prof. Schneller was familiar to find his team. He had the ability to his credit to lead the group with inspiration and ignition to the task. As a chemist and biochemist, to guide a group of chemists to their targets of course requires something unique what he had. Prof Schneller was a visionary to use error as opportunity to promote innovation in the field of Medicinal Chemistry.

The boy could feel the visual pleasure when got the crystals of a precursor from its pure syrup after twelve days of tiresome in situ work before the diene-dienophile cycloaddition proposed. He could not find words to express the offset, however, when the dienophile, benzyloxy acetylene did not work as per expectation. Instead, it underwent self rearrangement to indanone, a different but known compound, not of his interest. More than a month's effort appeared as if went to hell. American, Daryl Sauer, another PDA of Prof. Scheneller had shared the shock but encouraged to find an alternative what in fact had happened three months later in a different method for the same target as credential credit. The potential of the earlier method, the shortest but difficult is still to be tested positive. He could not find words to display his unrest in body mind and spirit for the whole night to observe a reaction, the last step to the target molecule called Pyrazofurin (β-anomer). The reaction was deprotection of benzyl group protecting hydroxyl group by Pd/H_2, Cyclohexene at 45 psi pressure in a still bomb. The curiosity of the boy to record NMR in a 600 MHz instrument is unforgettable. Mr Ron was very skilled to run the 90 MHz NMR machine in the training session of the boy. The environment for research was quite conducive to provoke innovation. Experiences there were opportunities what the boy had come with. From library to laboratory corridor people were busy to run after their assignment, no time to gossip. The underground auditorium was another source of attraction to the seminar or Ph.D defend before staff and students. The then Machintosh computer with laser printer in the laboratory core was more than busy with young scientists. The living view of Xing Chen towards enzyme, the boy could not digest. The neck tie presented by Jayu Wu as a token of love is still with him even after 30 years. Wendlin Frick, a German PDA, a path finder to boy's table in the laboratory was very often seen as if in a different world. Rita Sharma, Sharadbala Patil, Samala J Rao and Suhaib Siddiqui were with the boy in the Indian camp of PDAs. Masakaju Koga used to work at night to avoid clapping of the rest in case glassware broke down in day time. Anthony Gambino (shortly Tony) was relaxed with occasional interference of amusement. One day he asked the boy, "Can you please tell Dr. Pradhan, why so many Indians and Chinese are coming to U.S.A. in academics" ? The boy replied, "This is because they are being chosen better and therefore, being called". "No, that is not fact", said Tony. The boy said, "Then you tell me, what is fact that you think ?". Tony said, "They are coming because they are very hard workers". The boy felt elevated with this. However, in the very next moment Tony said, "But they accept very less pay". The boy then felt shame and pain as if got a slap at his cheek. Tony's last reply help showed the boy the path to India back. The dream of working in an Indian institute like IISc, IITs, CCMB, IICB and the like began to intensify after this incident. Six months before departure from United States, the boy was offered the post of instructor by Dr. Schneller himself. Unfortunately and humbly he had to say no and preferred instead to come back India after two years of stay.

Dr. Suhaib Siddiqi used to talk very less, quite often taking coffee was very keen to present the boy with a molecular model set while coming back home. He was very interactive and helpful by nature towards research as a team. After Dr. Schneller the boy liked to discuss with Dr. Siddiqi preferably when faced problem of difficulty in work. Dr. Siddiqi is now the VP of technology in chemistry and is driving ZS Genetics labeling work and assisting management with business planning. He is the top tier of nucleotide chemists in the world having extensive experience and success both as a medicinal chemist and as a computational chemist. The boy loved to work with Dr Siddiqi at a table next to his own.

Dr Rajani Kanta Behera, popular for Beheramine, an amine after him and Reader-on-leave at Sambalpur University was a PDA of Prof G. R. Newkome in the same floor of same Science Centre of University of South Florida, Tampa where the boy was working with Prof Schneller. The boy was feeling all along familiar with Dr. Behera and his family there in the same residential complex. The boy has enjoyed his time with Dr. Behera both in and off the laboratory either in Florida or outside. Dr Behera was a senior faculty of Sambalpur University where the boy has built his own student career from graduation onwards before U.S. assignment. The work hunger of the boy had in fact intensified by the continuous encouragement of Dr

Behera who is younger brother of Prof. Behera, the Ph.D. guide of the boy. The effort of Prof Behera in India to write a letter to Dr P. K. Jesthi, the then Director, Higher Education, Government of Orissa to sanction the study leave of the boy for the second year was commendable and provided timely support. The boy felt again reactive to listen from a flag seller in New York foot path. The message behind, "Because it is U.S. flag, its price is 2.5 dollars compared to that of Indian flag being 1 dollar in spite of same size and quality" was not acceptable to the boy. He purchased both with reluctance for the former that helped again to show him way back to India. The monopoly and dominance of American world over the rest besides European and Japanese finally chocked the boy's oxygen supply to force suffer from healthy respiration. This was enough to bring an end to his U.S. mission this time and initiate a new beginning for an Indian assignment.

With a new energetic mind setup and a lot of hope and dream, the boy left San Fransisco for the then Calcutta (now Kolkata) on 21st November 1991 in a Singapore Airlines plane. After joining back to his work left two years ago in Municipal College, Rourkela he continued to apply for an assignment with teaching and research scope in India itself. In his first attempt he approached Prof K. M. Madhyastha, Head, Department of Chemistry, IISc, Bangalore for possible guidance and direction to extend his work on nucleosides and nucleotides as a potential drug to check the malignant growth of viruses or to derive innovation out of it. Prof Madhyastha denied, however, did not dishearten the boy. He recommended the proposal to Prof K. N. Ganesh of NCL, Pune. Prof Ganesh was doing excellent work in Nucleic Acid Chemistry. For a quite long period he remained silent not only to the proposal but also to the correspondences of the boy who then thought to carry out the work of his dream in Orissa itself. After his marriage in 1995, he became bit distorted from the path of his research desire in India because of so many failures to find himself in a suitable position of teaching and research in all of the three core universities of Orissa and some national institutions like Centre for Cellular and Molecular Biology (CCMB), Hyderabad and Centre for Advanced technology (CAT), Indore. Till now he has never asked himself whether he has made the right decision to come back to India leaving US assignment so soon because this was his own decision free from ambiguity or overexcitement. His nearest hope was erstwhile REC (now NIT), Rourkela. This time he was squeezed by the REC official machinery not to be called for interview. On the contrary, less deserving (as per his assessment) local applicants were seen to be called for the same. To his personal enquiry, principal and departmental head played hide and sick and started throwing the ball to each other. Principal said that intimation for interview had been sent. After a few minutes he again said that short list without the boy had been made not by him but by departmental head who said that it was the work of principal not of him. In between, the boy was running from pillar to post for a genuine call letter which he felt to have deserved. However, nothing went as per expectation. He had to appeal to Governor of Orissa, with a copy to principal, REC, Rourkela. Without delay he was called by the registrar over telephone at 10.30 pm for interview next day at 3 pm. He, however, emphasized for the written call letter like REC had served to other applicants. Unfortunately, registrar expressed inability of REC administration to issue such call letter. So, the boy did not attend interview which was conducted in time as per schedule. The boy instead, filed a petition in the high court of Orissa. As a result, the outcome this interview stood null and void by the honorable high court. The boy was again not happy with such verdict of high court when the prayer was to give an opportunity to appear before interview. His unhappiness was conveyed to the concerned advocate whose reply was also not convincing to the boy. Subsequently the advertisement for the same post came again with specification of date of birth so that he could not even apply. The suffocation from these incidents was so intense that unfortunately he could not suffocate further for his dream in this premier institute of his home city. So, he had to surrender before Time and chain of government machinery.

Fortunately or unfortunately, in 2011 he was selected as the then Reader (now associate Professor) in Chemistry in Utkal University, Bhubaneswar on a contractual basis for a period of four years. In view of his long twenty two years of current regular service with full pension he, however, applied for two year lien instead of quitting the present service in order to join this newly selected job. Despite three examples of lien being granted to case like his own and no objection from Director, DHE, Bhubaneswar, the Governing Body in general, Principal in particular of Municipal College, Rourkela did not sanction the lien that he had applied. He, therefore, appealed to Honourable Governor of the state. To his belief the appeal is kept buried under political pressure, remained in dark till today and finally he could not fulfil his dream of research in Utkal University, Bhubaneswar too. Hopefully, he is predestined not to suffocate adequately to his dream study, but the fight would carry to energize in the coming days.

The selectivity of the boy to work in a particular field in particular place quite often narrowed the possibility of getting him absorbed into a position as per his expectation. But instead, it has pushed him to a higher altitude from where he could visualize a broader view necessary for higher ambition. In the mean time regional engineering college (REC), Rourkela, which is 12 km away from Municipal College was upgraded to National Institute of Technology (NIT) and its department of chemistry installed a 400 MHz NMR instrument that boosted the boy once again to go for some collaborative work with NIT. The boy was working with a minor research project of UGC amounting Rs. 1.5 Lakhs with himself as principal investigator (PI) and his colleague, Mrs Ashima Dash as Co-Investigator (Co-I). Municipal college was kind enough to provide space and arrangements like fume exhaust cupboard, nitrogen facility, oven, refrigerator, computer etc. for the research laboratory, in the Division of Organic Synthesis (DOS) of chemistry department in the college. The Western Orissa Development Corporation (WODC), Government of Orissa, extended its cooperation to provide the much needed rotavapour for research in the field. In fact, the minor research project that was already running was not a solution to the boy's dream project that necessarily needs good amount of funds and extra hands like research assistant (RA) and research fellow (RF). Looking at some demerits of the DOS, the boy first tried for execution of his interest in collaboration with NIT, Rourkela through Prof. Niranjan Panda and Prof. Raj Kishore Patel of NIT. However, it came out again a vain when NIT, Rourkela denied the proposed collaboration on the plea that Municipal College was too small to collaborate with

NIT, Rourkela. With this, the boy was definitely struck but not at all shrunk. Rather, he was strengthened in mind to proceed in yet another different way.

Mentioning the available infrastructural facilities for research in DOS of Municipal College, Rourkela and use of 400 MHz NMR for spectra on commercial basis, the spirited boy with himself as PI, Mrs Dash as Co-I and one junior research fellow (JRF), submitted a major research project amounting Rs. 12,59,000/- to the Department of Science and Technology (DST), Government of India on 22.02.2011 for approval. The project was, however, not considered for approval. Next year he resubmitted with reduced amount of Rs. 9,71,000/-. This time the project was successfully short listed for recommendation. The PI was called to Hyderabad to defend the project before the Program Advisory Committee (PAC) of the DST. Unfortunately the project was finally not recommended. It was not possible to take up a project in the field thought with much reduced price. So he took time to think over it. With this little success for being shortlisted, the boy after consultation with some established PIs known to him submitted on 30.01.2016 a modified project costing Rs. 24,99,501/- with one RF and one RA besides self as PI and Dr Ajay K. Mishra, another colleague of the DOS as Co-I. Again there was no success at the end. In connection with a measure research project in the DOS his were failed attempts. After three consecutive attempts within a span of five years had there been a success to get a major research project sanctioned, it would have given unexpected pleasure to his team and himself. Anyway, this grand failure could be attributed to many reasons like limited research potential of PI and infrastructure available at the DOS. Either the suffocation was not enough or the target was too difficult to reach at the DOS conditions by the persons proposed. So it remained unachievable so far and he continued to drown into the waters of opposition in spite of his efforts to come out in search of oxygen of success.

Municipal College, Rourkela established in 1978 is affiliated to Sambalpur University. It was attraction one day for many young talented individuals to serve as teaching faculty. The boy, therefore, opted with a vision. With a view to bringing glory and recognition at the national level, two national seminars sponsored by the UGC were successfully conducted by Municipal College, Rourkela with the boy as one of the two organizing secretaries. The experience, involvement and emotion that he has had will never be away from his mind. However, the vision that he has developed to introduce P.G. Course in chemistry department, to establish the DOS as a research centre recognized by the Sambalpur University and to organize an international seminar remained unfulfilled before his superannuation. Hope and wish, the job is left for the youngsters to come. In fact, it is suffocating to be surrounded by so many successes in the environment and not being able to catch one in the system. Moreover, suffocation today brings us the struggle necessary to develop the strength we need tomorrow.

Human desires are unlimited, so all may not be fulfilled. But the efforts behind remain rewarded directly or indirectly in terms of cash or kind that may not be perceived by him. He is a part of the Whole and is self incomplete for which he may not understand the consequence of his work. Therefore, he is to work only, without any demand for the result. Better, he is to leave the result to Him. The pleasure of continuous work as an instrument may be through pain is always within reach. He is to enjoy it.

'Suffocation from' brings 'suffocation for' which is a strength in the beginning to keep one moving and success at the end through failures to derive eternal pleasure and peace. A suffocating matter might have moved to life. A suffocating life is continually evolving and in a day may evolve to spirit. Continuous call from below and Blessing from above would evolve a life to sustain immortality on earth.

* * * * *

Epilogue

Nature, the teacher of teachers, the scientist of scientists, the laboratory of laboratories is created by the Almighty in the most delicate, subtle and suitable manner for smooth governance with peace and tranquility. Man continues to enjoy the status of the most developed creature in His creation. God has inducted in man the mind to think and act through brain and the conscience to have a control over mind for a balanced but persistent administration in His kingdom. However, human beings find today the right path in one direction to a limited length and the wrong avenues in many ways of unlimited measures. Why is it so when both mind and conscience evolve towards spirituality ?

Science, the brain child of man, encounters two possible factors affecting natural behaviour in matter. The statistical factor looks after the probability of quantitative happening while stability factor favours the comfortable change in matter. As a form of matter, Methane (CH_4) when undergoes thermal or photochemical chlorination in presence of chlorine in non-stoichiometric amounts, the fate of mono and polychlorinated products varies depending on the amounts of Methane and chlorine after continuous exposure to heat or light. When Methane is in excess, monochlorinated product (CH_3Cl) is major and polychlorinated products (CH_2Cl_2, $CHCl_3$, CCl_4) are minor and the reaction is guided by statistical factor. Therefore, more probable reaction does happen in quantitative manner as a matter of chance. On the other hand, in case of excess chlorine, the result is the reverse and is governed by stability factor. Reactions through more stable intermediates proceed to kinetically and thermodynamically more stable products as a matter of choice. Mind evolves statistically while conscience transforms kinetically and thermodynamically. Therefore, one is to be conscientious not to see the domination of mind over conscience.

To take part actively in the process of human evolution of both mind and conscience to supermind and supramental consciousness, we need energy-the energy to move. When the environment favours, we are blessed. However, when it opposes, we are rather more preferred to face a challenge to overcome which would give us pleasure that we don't find in the former. One is reminded of the lines of Shelley : "Our sincerest laughter with some pain is fraught." Success without failure is not a success in reality, but success through continuous fall and rise is the true success, as the proverb goes, "Failure is the pillar of success". Let us continue to cash on this finding with morale in the journey of matter to spirit/psyche/soul. Suffocation from limitation opens the door for a winner to suffocate for surplus. This in fact brings success without satisfaction and the process continues to infinity. Success of satisfaction, however, puts an end to move further. Once motion stops success becomes out of the reach. Of course, suffocation of today is, no doubt, a strength that provides necessary energy to fight singlehandedly the challenges of tomorrow and to keep one progressive throughout in a living style.

* * * * *

When in your work you find something giving trouble outside, look within and you will find in yourself the corresponding difficulty. Change yourself and the circumstances will change.
The Mother

"Insanity is doing the same thing over and again, but expecting different results"
Albert Einstein

"Live as if you were to die tomorrow. Learn as if you were to live forever"
Mahatma Gandhi

"No matter how busy you may think you are, you must find time for reading, or surrender yourself to self-chosen ignorance"
Atwood H Townsend

www.ingramcontent.com/pod-product-compliance
Ingram Content Group UK Ltd.
Pitfield, Milton Keynes, MK11 3LW, UK
UKHW042001230426
12048UKWH00009B/470

9 789353 479046